Charlotte tugged him down toward her.

He went willingly, wrapping his hands around her back.

"This is just to shut you up," she told him.

Declan's own mouth curved in an answering smile.

He kissed her deeper. There wasn't an inch of space between them and he liked that. He lost himself in a kiss that was better than anything he'd ever felt before.

When he finally pulled back, her eyes were closed, a flush of pink on her cheeks, all of her soft and trusting. He held on to her, not ready to let go.

"Wow." She bit her lower lip when they finally pulled back and stared at each other. "That was something. It's a good thing we got that out of our systems."

As if. He smoothed her hair back from her face. "We're not done. All you have to do is tell me what you want. Anything you want."

Dear Reader,

"Cinderella" is my guilty pleasure. Prince Charming, the most popular, fabulously wealthy man, falls in love with a hardworking, optimistic, down-on-her-luck woman. He comes with a castle accessory! Even better—writes she who buys far too many clothes imagining places to wear them—Cinderella gets a glamorous (and free!) makeover with hair, shoes and a ball gown.

Charlotte Palsgrave isn't looking for Prince Charming when movie star Declan Masterson makes a guest appearance in her life. She's too busy cleaning up after a failed relationship and a really, really bad year at work. But Declan recognizes the someone special Charlotte hides behind the quiet facade and the plain clothes—and he wants the whole world to see her, too. So he makes her a deal: he'll provide the makeover and she'll get the resources she needs to take care of a very large problem at work.

But like Cinderella, what appeals most is that Charlotte doesn't ever change fundamentally. She's still a strong, bright, optimistic woman dealing with the challenges life sends her way—and she comes out on top and makes her own happily-ever-after. And along the way, it may just so happen that Declan's heart undergoes the biggest, most magical makeover of them all.

Happy reading,

Anne Marsh

ANNE MARSH

THE INHERITANCE TEST

HARLEQUIN
DESIRE

Recycling programs for this product may not exist in your area.

ISBN-13: 978-1-335-58165-5

The Inheritance Test

For questions and comments about the quality of this book, please contact us at CustomerService@Harlequin.com.

Harlequin Enterprises ULC
22 Adelaide St. West, 41st Floor
Toronto, Ontario M5H 4E3, Canada
www.Harlequin.com

Printed in U.S.A.

Anne Marsh writes sexy contemporary and paranormal romances, because the world can always enjoy one more alpha male. She started writing romance after getting laid off from her job as a technical writer—and quickly decided happily-ever-afters trumped software manuals. She lives in North Carolina with her two kids and five cats.

Books by Anne Marsh

Harlequin Desire

The Inheritance Test

Harlequin Dare

Ruled
Inked
Her Intern
Hot Boss
Hookup
Have Me
Hold Me

Visit the Author Profile page
at Harlequin.com for more titles.

You can also find Anne Marsh on Facebook,
along with other Harlequin Desire authors,
at Facebook.com/HarlequinDesireAuthors!

For Lillie (and Pinto and Ava).
Your tweets are a very bright,
happy light in my week.
Thank you!

One

"Prove you're Masterson material in the next ninety days or you're out."

Declan Masterson had never backed down from a challenge in his life, but this one was a shock.

In the years since his adoptive father J.J. had plucked him and his brother Nash from foster care, dropping them into the exotic world of Hollywood, J.J. had blustered and threatened whenever Declan had failed to live up to the illustrious Masterson standard of a ruthless Hollywood player. In the past, Declan had responded to J.J.'s criticism by going off on another of his wild adventures, but he'd turned over a new, reformed leaf when J.J. had finally named him as his heir apparent.

"You'd better define *out*." He sprawled in his chair, watching J.J. carefully. J.J. looked relaxed in his white shirt with the sleeves rolled up, suit jacket discarded, but underestimating him was like mixing up snakes and celebrities in Hollywood's famous Runyon Canyon. You only made that mistake once.

"Fired," J.J. snapped back. "No longer provisional CEO of Masterson Entertainment. I have an offer to buy this company—and they don't need you."

Much as he pretended it didn't, J.J.'s criticism stung. Declan's jaw tightened involuntarily. He'd spent two years under J.J.'s thumb earning the chance to run the family company, to green-light his own projects and make films that would change people's lives. Despite years learning moviemaking from the ground up—because J.J. would hand him nothing and he earned it or did without—now it could all be taken away.

Because he wasn't, and never had been, a true Masterson.

"I've tripled our revenues," he pointed out. "I'm damned good at what I do. We both know it."

Masterson Entertainment produced films in partnership with other major film studios and was about to ink another multi-film cofinancing deal. While Declan could walk away and start his own film studio— his acting career had earned him millions—he'd have to give up projects he felt passionately about if J.J. followed through on his threat to sell. He'd have to start over from nothing.

He'd vowed he'd never be nothing again.

J.J. pinned him with a glare. "You've made a joke of the Masterson name with your adventures. In the last two years, you've free-climbed the tallest casino in Las Vegas, headlined a Megavalanche bike race in the Alps and dove with great white sharks."

He'd also run the company and, in the year prior to

that, made a blockbuster movie that had outperformed its projected revenue at the box office. Those contributions were outweighed by his reputation as the playboy prince of film.

Declan couldn't explain the restlessness that constantly drove him. He simply had to lose himself in intense, thrilling activities. It was a drive that he'd—mostly—channeled into his career as one of Hollywood's leading action heroes, and now into Masterson Entertainment. But since he could only be on set so much, he also climbed, skied and raced as fast as he could. The more extreme the conditions, the more he loved it. In the past few years he'd earned a reputation as a fierce competitor in the world's top sailing races. And when there wasn't a race or a film or a business deal to be made, yes, there were women.

"Those things would be fine," J.J. continued, since clearly *his* definition of *fine* was the only one that mattered, "in moderation. Instead, you turn everything into a spectacle, with a film crew, ridiculous bets and women. You proposed to an actress by scaling the wall to her hotel balcony. You did this at midnight, in boxer briefs and with a candy ring from a gas station."

Declan grinned. "Harry Winston was closed, so I improvised. You left out the part where she refused and the paparazzi caught the whole thing on camera."

He'd fallen off the respectability wagon rather publicly that night in Beverly Hills, but it had been funny, at least until the photos had surfaced and his impulsivity had been commemorated in the tabloids and on dozens of celebrity gossip websites.

Proposing to Jessie St. Chiles, his costar in his last film, had been an impulse. They'd been friends with

benefits, but Declan knew he wasn't marriage material. His own biological father had walked out early
and J.J.'s wife had divorced him after just six months
of marriage. She'd been long gone before Declan and
Nash had arrived at the Malibu mansion. Jessie knew
he wasn't actually looking to get married and they'd
both had a good laugh.

"When people hear your name, they wonder what
ludicrous stunt you'll pull next," J.J. growled.

"Which is very on-brand for us."

J.J.'s face darkened. "It is—for our film talent and
our marketing department. But when you were racing
in the Alps two months ago, you were off-grid for two
weeks. Our cofinancing deal went bad and we lost a
ten-picture deal because no one could find the CEO.
You've spent more time out of the office than in. No one
takes you seriously in the boardroom because the only
time we can count on you to show up is for the start of
a race. You're no Masterson."

"Not by birth," he agreed. J.J. had adopted him and
Nash at the ages of eight and six. J.J.'s own biological
son was estranged. Depending on who told the story,
Revere had either left the Malibu mansion at seventeen
or been kicked out. Either way, he hadn't been heard
from since.

J.J. flipped a photograph across the desk. The camera had caught the woman in the picture off guard, her
eyes half-closed, lips parted. Late twenty-something
with brown hair pulled back in an unremarkable ponytail, she wore a boring, white polo shirt with an em-
broidered logo. *Martha's Kids*.

"This is the daughter of Bryant Palsgrave, a successful Wall Street investor from one of New England's old-

est families. Wealthy. Discreet. Her brother could be a future president."

"Charming," he said dryly, unsure of J.J.'s angle.

That kind of stultifying, quiet lifestyle was a pretty prison. Fortunately, old money families wouldn't have anything to do with someone like him, an actor, recklessly decadent and from a working-class background that J.J.'s adoption could never compensate for. Declan had no problem working his ass off—he'd spent his twenties building his film career, starting as a stuntman and then moving into feature film acting. He'd made a lot of money and been on the cover of magazines, but now he wanted to produce.

Growing up in Malibu, his neighbors had all been in the industry: movie stars, producers, screenwriters, musicians. The gated homes might cost north of seven million dollars, but when your kid went down the street to play, the mantel held an Oscar or Golden Globe. Bodyguards and luxury cars, with paparazzi lurking behind the well-manicured palm trees and dodging the dog walkers to the stars, were the norm. As a working class transplant, Declan had been shocked and then enchanted. He'd yearned to be part of those beautiful people with a magnetism and presence that marked them as members of a powerful Hollywood tribe.

J.J. followed the headshot with a glossier sheet of paper, a press release for a New England boat race that made Declan laugh. The participants were sailing two-person keelboats, just twenty-two feet long with a shallow draft and one mast. He'd raced faster and bigger when he'd been a teenager.

"The race around Martha's Vineyard next month raises funds for charity. One local and one celebrity per boat. The fastest boat wins the million-dollar prize for the charity of their choice. Charlotte Palsgrave needs a partner and I owe her father a favor."

"You're joking," he snapped. He raced million-dollar yachts with a full crew in the world's most extreme weather conditions. No way would he partner with a spoiled, local, blue-blooded princess in what amounted to a glorified dinghy.

J.J. leaned forward, steepling his fingers. "You will partner with Charlotte and win this race for her—and you will be the perfect Masterson representative. Charming, well-bred, disciplined. There will be no scandals. You will prove, once and for all, that you are a worthy heir to the Masterson legacy and that I can count on you to be where you're needed. In exchange, I will refuse the buyout offer I have and will sign Masterson Entertainment over to you. You'll own it, lock, stock and barrel, and you will have sole control."

It was just a race, he told himself, and not even a hard one. One lap around Martha's Vineyard, some photo ops with the blue-blooded princess and he'd be on his way back to Hollywood with the real prize: his inheritance.

"Win this race," J.J. said. "And it's all yours."

Declan didn't know why J.J. had decided to finally back his bid to lead the family company—or why he'd consider selling the precious Masterson film studio. J.J. had a pathological need to be in control. And he loved nothing better than designing a series of challenges for "his boys," challenges that only underscored how unworthy he thought they were of whatever prize he'd dangled before them. Nash had walked away from J.J.'s tests five years ago, immersing himself in his oil and chemical company. Declan had done the same—until

two years ago, when he'd given into temptation and returned. The only thing that had made it tolerable was
knowing he could see the finish line—a line that J.J.
had just moved. Could he still win this? He thought he
could—but he'd also learned a thing or two during his
years in Hollywood. One of the most important lessons?
Always, *always* get the deal in writing.

"Draw up a contract," he said. "Thirty days. In exchange for no bad publicity and one race win, I get
Masterson Entertainment."

He wouldn't lose.

Two

Prince Charming and the wallflower, Charlotte Palsgrave told herself. *You know how this story goes.* But truth was she didn't. Not anymore. Anxiety had her wallflower self twisted up in well-deserved knots. She swallowed the boulder-sized lump in her throat because if she cried now where people could see her, her secret would come out. For months she'd dreaded discovery and part of her wanted to stand up and scream the truth. To admit *I'm sorry.* She'd made a disastrous mistake that she regretted with all her heart. This race was her very last chance to fix the damage before it irrevocably hurt other people, so she really, *really* needed Prince Charming to get on board with her make-up plan. If she'd known just how badly off course life could get, she would have planned better.

Invested in a pair of kick-ass glass slippers…

Just in case she'd secretly acquired a fairy godmother, she double-checked her feet. Nope. Her ever-so-practical navy blue sneakers hadn't been magically transformed. She was still on her own. It was times like this that she couldn't quite shut out her father's disapproving voice in her head, a loud, critical voice that she'd never managed to measure up to or please. She'd gotten better at ignoring the voice or even occasionally talking back to it, but that hard-won confidence vanished when she faced a social situation like today's. Not only was she standing at Martha's Vineyard's most exclusive yacht club, but she'd voluntarily agreed to get in a boat in three weeks, race at unspeakable speeds through open ocean off the coast of Massachusetts and do it all in the company of a celebrity Prince Charming, aka Declan Masterson, aka her new nemesis because she desperately needed to win the million-dollar prize and he refused to get onboard with her plans.

Magicking up a pair of glass slippers would have been easier.

Mostly because while she preferred to color neatly within the lines, guided by her master plan and a binder bristling with sticky notes, Declan preferred to careen at full speed in random directions.

Worse, while he looked like a hero on the outside, he was one-hundred-percent nefarious villain on the inside.

She slanted a glance at where he stood, surrounded by an admiring crowd of yachties and media. This was only partly due to his celebrity status as a Hollywood star and acting CEO of a blockbuster film studio— and mostly due to the man's sheer animal chemistry. He channeled rugged today, his wavy blond hair tousled from tugging his fingers through it. Hazel eyes,

a stubble-roughened, firm jaw and the man's mouth…
Well. It was honestly a blessing that when he opened
his mouth what came out had her seeing red, because
otherwise she would have stopped and stared because
the man was a work of art and she felt a sensual tug
when she was close. That was a first for her, that overwhelming awareness of a man, the curiosity about what
it would be like to get closer. A whole lot closer.

He must have made some kind of Mephistophelian
deal with the devil for that charm he turned on and off
at will.

Just be glad that they're taking his *picture and not
yours.* The YouTube videos she'd watched on master-
ing selfie poses seemed entirely inadequate as Declan
flashed a killer grin at the nearest lens. *Doesn't matter.*
She had zero interest in competing for Miss Photogenic
in this beauty pageant. She froze in front of a camera.
Her life didn't revolve around pictures and social media
and she valued that. She worked behind-the-scenes as
the director of the nonprofit Martha's Kids, creating
summer camps for foster kids so they could swim and
kayak, swap friendship bracelets and enjoy lighthearted
fun. Camp had been her own escape from a less-than-
idyllic childhood home, so she loved making the magic
happen for these kids.

"Charlotte," her golden-haired nemesis called. "Join
us."

Her feet moved automatically because the man had
his own gravitational pull. Oh, God. She was doomed.
Resist.

She stopped walking and deployed her secret weapon:
the truth. "You don't need me over there. Thanks any-
ways."

Then she smiled because politeness mattered. Declan stared at her thoughtfully. *Great, okay, move right along, big guy.* Most people looked right through her, their gaze skipping over her very ordinary face and the medium-length brown hair she always pulled into a ponytail. She didn't bother with makeup beyond a moisturizer with SPF and her wardrobe consisted of yoga wear and comfortable shoes. She might be dismissed as boring, but she loved herself and felt safe. That was all that mattered.

Okay, so she *had* felt safe, until her ex-fiancé had vanished, taking with him her dreams, along with most of Martha's Kids' annual operating budget. As a result, she'd pulled strings to enter the race that took place in three weeks since, despite his flaws, her father was a prominent Vineyard local. She'd lucked out with her random partner. Declan's pretty face and celebrity standing would rake in donations during these pre-race events because people fell over themselves to make a man like him happy. Plus, he actually knew how to sail a boat. He was a guaranteed winner and that prize money would make up her budgetary shortfall— *if* she could ever get him to agree to picking Martha's Kids as their charity.

"Come on, darling." He winked, fully aware no woman would deny him. Handsome and hot, yada yada. *Pay no attention*, she told her hormones. "You make my day brighter and we're partners."

She snorted. She preferred to think of their arrangement as a sixty/forty split where she handled decision-making and responsibilities while he looked glamorous and expensive. That division of labor played to both their strengths. "Three weeks until race day. Tick, tick,

Hollywood. I'll meet you at the boat for a practice run when you're done posing."

He shook his head and held out a strong, sun-bronzed hand to her. He wore faded board shorts and a white T-shirt that hugged his muscled chest and framed a whole lot of masculine strength. The tousled hair, warm eyes and stubble screamed, *I just rolled out of bed and don't you wonder who was there with me?*

Which she didn't. She went one worse and imagined herself in that bed, possibly a fantasy bed in the luxury hotel where he'd held off terrorists in his last box-office hit. He'd had a memorable moment with his leading lady in that movie, one where they'd celebrated being very much not dead by ripping each other's clothes off. Carefully, she looked away from him, aiming her gaze at his feet in case he could tell from her face that she was imagining him naked.

It was just a Prince Charming side effect, one that would pass when she broke free of his orbit.

"One quick picture," she bit out, ignoring his hand. He wouldn't move on to the next agenda item until he was ready, and to win this race, she needed practice— lots of practice and exposure therapy in the measly three weeks before race day. Unlike Declan, who was a world-class racer with wins in exotic locations like Malta, the Route du Rhum in France and all parts of the Caribbean, she had a love-hate relationship with the ocean. While she'd happily admire it from the beach, she'd almost drowned the last time she'd gotten too close.

Declan wiggled the fingers on his outstretched hand. *Ugh.* If he actually crooked a finger at her, she'd give felony murder serious consideration. *Just win the race and save your kids and* then *you can kill him.*

So she hotfooted it across the deck, stopping awkwardly next to him. Even at five foot nine in her bare feet, the man had six inches on her. Declan took charge, effortlessly and with a great deal of charm. He slung a casual arm around her shoulders, tugging her into his side and turning them both to face the photographers. Cameras clicked and then he dropped his arm, stepping away. She didn't mind, she told herself. When someone protested, he shook his head.

"The lady said one." He snagged a white linen shirt from the chair where he'd tossed it and pulled it on over his T-shirt. The expensive Rolex watch he'd won in his last race glinted in the summer sun as he slipped his sunglasses on.

From the crowd of his admirers, a reporter asked the inevitable. "Have you decided which charity to sponsor?"

She opened her mouth, but Declan beat her, flashing the man a warm smile. "We're committed to an animal charity."

"*We* haven't decided yet," she growled. Not that the media pack paid attention. Nope. They were watching Prince Charming button his shirt. "Martha's Kids is obviously my first choice. We'll be sure to let you know."

Naturally, Declan heard her.

He just wouldn't *listen*. He'd suggested six different animal charities, each more ridiculously specific than the last.

"Let's discuss and revisit." He winked at her again— was it too much to hope his eye got stuck that way?— and set off with a long-legged, way-too-sexy stride.

Darn it. That meant he'd get to their as-yet-unnamed

boat first and then he'd take command of the tiller just like he took command of everything.

If she were a braver woman, she'd shove the man sauntering down the dock into the water. One surge of speed plus a quick shoulder check and *boom*, six feet three inches of muscled, sun-kissed, way-too-arrogant male would hit the oil-slicked, briny flotsam bobbing around the boats in the marina. Surely even Declan Masterson's Hollywood good looks couldn't survive that swim unscathed. If she weren't so invested in winning their boat race in three weeks, she'd do it. Maybe. Okay, so almost probably definitely not because she generally believed in being nice and keeping things calm, and nice people didn't push a man into the water and make a scene.

Even if that man totally deserved it.

Future Charlotte moved *dunk Declan Masterson* to the top of the bucket list she'd tackle after she won this race and fixed her mistake.

Everything had all happened so fast: handsome and funny, George Moore had wowed the board of Martha's Kids during his interview six months earlier and afterward he'd been so eager to work with her. She'd handed over the reins of their accounting to him, had failed to double-check him because he'd seemed so perfect. They'd enjoyed a special connection, or so she'd believed. He'd wined and dined her with a series of romantic dates to the Vineyard's flashiest spots.

Caught up in the whirlwind romance and knocked off-balance by the outgoing George's obvious interest in her quieter, shyer self, she hadn't questioned his motivations. It was friendship, attraction, a lightning-bug spark of attraction. After mere weeks, he'd declared his love and suggested they go diamond shopping. Her father had flat-out stated that a man who looked like a Greek god would never be interested in a plain-Jane girl like her. And his totally expected criticism had made her decide that for once she'd dig in her heels and live.

Which had turned out to be a big mistake. *Huge.* Because six months after he'd blown into Martha's Vineyard, George had slipped away without any of the fanfare he loved so much—and he'd cleaned out not only her bank account but Martha's Kids' as well. She'd been thinking *romance* and he—well, he'd thought *smoke screen.* The embezzlement would become public knowledge when the district attorney filed charges shortly. Nothing stayed secret forever. This race was her ticket to repairing the damage George had done because the prize money would refill the foundation's coffers even if it could never erase her guilt.

She concentrated on the sun-warmed planks of the dock stretching away in front of her. Mooring posts jutted up out of the salt water and were decorated with seagulls. Despite the sky's perfect shade of blue, the warmth of the sun didn't work its usual magic on the tension that had the muscles in her shoulders knotting. Breaking into an undignified trot, she caught up with Declan, trying not to think about the ocean that she'd soon be sailing on.

"Charlotte." He slanted her a look she couldn't interpret. "What is your problem?"

"Why do I have to have a problem?"

His eyes danced. "You're clearly upset. Let's fix this."

She shook her head. "Is everything easy for you? No, don't answer. I've got a great idea. How about we stay on schedule and nominate our charity?"

"I've made multiple suggestions. You've shot them all down." He made it sound as if she were the illogical member of their team when the opposite was true.

"Your suggestions were ridiculous," she gritted out.

"So, convince me. Here I am, entirely, completely yours." He threw out his arms. "Why does Martha's Kids matter so much to you?"

Jeez. "Because I direct it? Because those foster kids deserve a summer of cabins, kayaks and crafts? Because *you* want to donate a million dollars of prize money to rescuing guinea pigs, which has to be a joke?"

He lifted one powerful shoulder in a shrug. "Guinea pigs are awesome."

"Not a million dollars' worth of awesome." Giving up on dignity, she speed-walked down the dock. Their two-person boat was at the very end, just to better mess with her head.

Declan's husky chuckle floated after her. *Ugh.* He was never serious. Toeing off her boat shoes, she sidled up to the edge of the dock. And froze. One step down. One big step down, minding the gap and the water—

"Nice try." Warm hands wrapped around her waist, shifting her gently to the side, and she bit back a squeal. Mostly. She was ticklish. Okay, and something else, a sizzle she wasn't willing to admit even to herself as he effortlessly moved her out of his way. Her arm brushed his side.

"Cheater," she hissed.

His mouth brushed her ear. "Takes one to know one."

He couldn't possibly know. No one knew. Not yet.

With another chuckle, he jumped down into the boat. Not for the first time she wished the charitable folks of Martha's Vineyard had belonged to any club other than the yacht club. Golfing, badminton, even bird-ing—why couldn't the prize be for the team who spot-ted the most herons? Water slapped against the dock, the waves darker blue and deep. At least the answer to her problem ex wasn't platform diving. She didn't have to put her face in. *Count your blessings.*

"One step at a time." Declan held out his hand to help her in. "You want to tell me why you don't like water but you've volunteered for a boat race?"

Even if she had been in the habit of sharing her fears with a complete stranger, she wouldn't have told him the truth. She wasn't sure she could, not after so many years of keeping quiet and pretending that everything was *fine*. So she went on the offensive.

"I'm fine. Why don't you tell me why you're head-lining a no-name boat race for charity instead of living your Hollywood best life?"

Three

Charlotte Palsgrave liked to pretend that everything was fine. But Declan was trained to pay attention to his opponent's body language in a fight and right now everything about his new partner screamed *anxious*.

Slightly rude.

And…unexpectedly sexy. Not that he had noticed. Much. The only time Charlotte didn't try to fade into the background was when they fought, and so far, she'd limited even those fights to brief verbal jabs and sideways glances. She didn't like him.

At all.

Insta-hate was a first. Most people focused on the wealth he wore like a shield or the surface excitement of his Hollywood success. They wanted stories about famous people, the inside scoop on the decadent Malibu parties and the vicarious buzz from hearing how he'd get out of a studio car and fans would roar as the cameras went off. They had to actually get to know him to be disappointed by who he was and to realize that he was simply playing the part he'd been cast in. Charlotte, however, had been disdainful from the first. She'd dismissed him as a pretty package that she couldn't be bothered to unwrap.

He was good at shucking off criticism thanks to the constant public scrutiny. If she also felt the desire that ate at him when he saw her, she covered it up well, directing only dislike his way, along with impatience and annoying superiority. He, on the other hand, couldn't keep his mind on the upcoming race. When he was around her, he wanted to kiss the tight line of her mouth, nip at the plush lower lip until she opened up and let him all the way in. She might not like drawing attention to herself and she might not be beautiful in the sparkling way that drew photographers and a crowd of admirers, but she was something, alright. His craving for her was a problem.

"Sit." He handed her a life jacket and pointed to the spot where she could get least in the way, ignoring her muttered *woof*.

While she fumed, flipping through the color-coded binder she clung to like a mooring line, he got them underway for their practice session. Guiding twenty feet of sailboat past slips filled with expensive luxury boats and out into open water was child's play, but he wanted to fine-tune their rig and get some more average headings for their tacks.

He'd met a lot of gorgeous women but Charlotte was different. Entirely too prickly, as well as stubborn and determined to make his life hell, but suddenly he knew what people meant when they said that "beauty was only skin-deep." Objectively, her looks were nothing out of the ordinary—brown hair, brown eyes, too curvy to fit into a sample size. But there was something about her that he liked looking at.

Martha's Vineyard skimmed by, all creamy sand and expensive beach cottages, as the boat's sails filled and she picked up speed. The familiar beat of wind on canvas and the play of water on the hull was invigorating, but he still couldn't quite believe he was once again dancing to his adoptive father's tune, vying to win his inheritance test. Except...

Charlotte Palsgrave was perfect window dressing.

He thought about that while he took them out into the open water, their little boat skimming over the waves. A feminine inhale, quickly stifled, shifted his attention from the ocean to his companion. She had a death grip on her binder, her eyes fixed unwaveringly on the horizon.

Reaching over, he pried the binder free and tucked it in the waterproof compartment beneath his legs. She promptly transferred her grip to the lifeline by her shoulder. "You okay?"

"Wonderful." She didn't look at him.

He was pretty certain that she'd just as soon tie the anchor to his ankle and drop him overboard in some convenient stretch of water as admit that racing and open ocean made her nervous. As far as he could tell, she made it through their daily practices on sheer determination.

And keeping secrets...

The only thing she didn't keep secret was her dislike

of him and he had weeks before he could claim victory and head back to California.

"You're the one who wants to discuss things—here's your opportunity."

"You want to talk *now*?"

"We could stop and swim," he teased.

She winced. "Let's pick our charity. It's Martha's Kids. Not hedgehogs or guinea pigs or whatever other animal you decided needed rescuing."

"Come on, darling," he said. "You need me to agree."

Martha's Kids seemed like a fine organization, especially given his own background as a foster child. The optics were great. But playing J.J.'s inheritance game was boring if necessary and arguing with Charlotte was shaping up to be his one note of excitement.

"You're asking me to be the good guy here," he continued.

"Some of us clearly lean more toward the bad end of the scale," she muttered.

He liked to win, and while he didn't cheat or hurt others to do so, he also went all in on his goals. He left everything out there on the playing field and sometimes he stepped on some toes in the process. So no, he wasn't a *good guy*.

"What can you offer me?" He leaned back, crossing his arms over his chest.

"It's charity." She briefly threw up her hands before seizing the lifeline again. "Why is everything about you, Hollywood? I know you live for attention and adventure, but some of us are trying to do the right thing. Maybe you could try to be different? Just this once?"

He was sick and tired of being told to change because who he was wasn't good enough. Maybe she should try it. He bet she'd hate it every bit as much as he did. In fact—

There was nothing Charlotte hated more than being the center of attention. Her reluctance to put herself forward gave him an idea.

"Since I'll be doing something that runs counter to my nature, it's only fair you do the same."

She looked at him, suspicion painting her face. "Like what?"

"I change—and you change," he said. "If I become a good guy and support Martha's Kids, you stop hiding in the shadows you love so much. You get a makeover. Hollywood-style. Hair, makeup, the works. I'll teach you everything I know about being a star. And when you're the belle of the ball on race night, I'll make sure Martha's Kids gets that million-dollar check. Do we have a deal?"

Declan Masterson could take a long walk off a short pier, and oh look, there was a handy dock at the marina just waiting for the king of Hollywood to take his fashion walk.

"That's a terrible deal. Why would I hand you another opportunity to humiliate me?"

Her nemesis crossed his arms and leaned forward. When he spoke his voice had the whiskey-rough cadence that had made the man famous. "Because you want me to give a million dollars to your charitable foundation."

"I'll earn it," she muttered. "I have to put up with you for an entire month."

"So a month alone with a movie star on the water is a hardship? Do you know how many people would take your place?" His jaw tightened. "You weren't picked for this boat, darling, because you're the director of Martha's Kids. You're here because your dear old dad is on the yacht club board and wants the locals to represent."

"Don't forget how much he likes winning." Her face heated. It wasn't untrue, but at least she'd got the world-champion sailor when the race committee had done the blind draws for partners.

"No one enjoys losing. Not that you would know anything about that, Princess."

Was the guy for real? "I lose all the time, so I can tell you from personal experience that, yes, it sucks and, yes, I prefer to avoid it. I don't know what your problem is, Hollywood. I'm here to raise money for a nonprofit that tries to erase the gap between people who have everything and people who have nothing."

He laughed. "With arts and crafts projects and campfires? Is there a special gold medal for sentimentality?"

She shot to her feet but had to sit back down again hard when she remembered how close she was to the water. Indignation and boats paired as poorly as Cheetos and white wine—or herself and this Hollywood charmer lounging on this stupidly small boat as if it were a movie set and she was a stand-in. No. Wait. In this metaphor, she was the person who fetched coffee and never got credit for the movie magic.

Although she could see why he was the source of that magic. He took up so much space, his big body relaxed, the wind playing with his hair as he radiated an easy confidence despite the open ocean surrounding them. Nothing knocked him off-balance and he didn't seem to know how unusual that was.

"I'm in this race for the right reasons," she insisted, double-checking the closure on her life jacket.

"And what reasons would those be?" He flashed her a teasing grin.

She revised her push-Declan-Masterson-into-the-water plan, speeding up the timeline. Push now, race later.

"I'm doing this for my kids. Not for you. Not for anyone else. For *them*. This is Jimmy." She whipped out her phone and pulled up a picture. "He likes the cabins because they're quiet and no one got shot last summer. And here's Jay. He doesn't get three meals a day when he's at home and unlimited hot dogs are his idea of heaven." She thumbed to another picture. "And this is Maggie. Like Jimmy and Jay, she's also not a cute little guinea pig. She's a ten-year-old girl who wants one summer to act like she's ten rather than ten-going-on-forty because she has a mother with severe depression who can't always get out of bed."

What she didn't add was that the best apologies came with a make-up plan, and only a million dollars could make up for what George had stolen. No matter how many times she said "I'm sorry" to the staff at Martha's Kids, the board and her kids, those were only words. Important words, but still.

"Charlotte—" He closed his eyes briefly and groaned. Funny how the real-life man was so different from the action heroes he played on the big screen. She liked that made-up man so much more. *He* saw a problem and he jumped in to fix it. "—are you really, truly doing this for the children?"

"Mostly," she said, because she had a no-lying policy, and pride and not disappointing her father had also factored into her decision to participate in the race. Martha's Vineyard was her home and screwing up on her home turf felt a million times worse than if she'd done the same in New York City or Boston—in any place, really, that she could run home from.

The smile spreading across his handsome face spelled trouble. "Still not convinced to be Team Martha's Kids. Are you sure you're not just in this for a shot at me?"

That was—

Her mouth hung open. The man was unbelievable. "Explain to me how your movie star awesomeness is all the motivation I need to be out here in the world's smallest boat on the world's biggest ocean?"

"Second-largest," he corrected. "The Atlantic is the second-largest ocean. You should get your facts straight, Charlotte. Admit that you like me," he crooned. "Just a little. Tell me the truth."

"Oh, my God. No."

"You're such a liar," he said cheerfully. "Completely full of shit. I'm not sure I should like that about you."

"I do not like you. This not some big sexual come-on, you ass." Did no one tell this man *no*? She gave him another irritated glance. Doing something seemed important, so she shuffled her butt down the seat so she could hang on to the side and poke at the steering stick thing at the same time.

The stupid boat didn't change course, though. She tugged on the stick—*tiller*—but it remained locked in place. Declan winked at her. Right. She tried for a better grip but since he wouldn't move out of her way, she had to reach over him, her life jacket bumping against his chest and side.

Whoa. He smelled good. Not that she was deliberately sniffing the man, but it was impossible not to notice. The piney, woodsy scent had to be cologne, but the rest of it—clean and male—was all him. And while she might like that scent far too much, it in no way meant she liked the *man*. How could he look so much like the screen god she might—*might*—have had one or two— or a thousand—fantasies about when the real-life person was such a disappointment?

"Are you sure? About not liking me?" He folded his hands behind his head, leaning helpfully back and out of her way. He also gave the tiller a quick nudge with his knee. Dammit. The boat moved.

"Quite," she bit out. "I'm sure *someone* has told you by now. The Vineyard loves a juicy piece of gossip, and although my relationship ended *slightly* less publicly than your last relationship, it was public enough. My fiancé ran away rather than marry me. I'm on a dating hiatus until my ovaries start sending notice. No one will think we're anything but race partners. You're entirely safe."

He frowned. "He dumped you."

"Quickly and quite publicly." And that wasn't even the worst of it.

His frown deepened. "So we actually have something in common. Do we have a deal? I'll play the good guy and throw my support behind your foundation. And you'll do the makeover."

She didn't trust his smile.

"It'll be fun." He flashed her a grin.

Danger.

"There's nothing wrong with me."

He made a rough noise, more growl than not, and tugged her in front of him. His legs bracketed hers and that put her practically on the man's lap. She started to protest but then he set her hands on the tiller, his closing over hers, moving hers. Show and tell.

"Move left to go right. Right to go left. Keep the changes small and smooth." The smooth wood sliding underneath her hands almost distracted her from the feel of Declan's hands covering hers. "There's nothing wrong with you. But we both need to reinvent our public selves, yeah? People see me and they think Romeo on a balcony. They see you and they remember George the asshole. This race could be a fresh start for both of us."

He unwrapped himself from her and shifted up the boat to balance their weight. Her heart pounded, her face flushing—from the way the boat rocked until he settled, she told herself. And not because watching Declan got her going.

"You really think a makeover will help me support Martha's Kids." She nudged the tiller to the left.

"I do."

"You realize that sounds completely ridiculous, right?"

"People will pay more attention. Some of them will be curious, while others will believe that if you look and act the part, you know what you're doing."

"So you're saying confidence is key." She squinted at him. "My first-grade teacher put that on the wall of our classroom."

"Still true," he said.

He flashed her another smile, this one genuine. The good humor and warmth in his grin had her wanting to agree, so clearly she hadn't fixed her man picker yet. It was all sign-me-up in the face of Declan's charm.

He winked at her, eyes bright with amusement. "Say yes."

Her heart turned over. Did that *flutter* thing.

Not a chance. NO.

There was nothing likable about this man. He was all surface charm and no depth. At least if she forgot that truth, he'd remind her the next time he opened his mouth.

"Do we have a deal?" He gestured toward the tiller and she sighed. Right. They were probably sailing toward Cuba or Madagascar. Since that was more ocean time than she was ready for, she made room for him and he took over. And let's face it, she was grateful for his easy confidence.

Grateful and a little turned on. She'd learn how to do this sailing thing if it killed her, but it had been a long day and there was a cheeseburger calling her name. Pie, too, if the local bakery truck hadn't sold out. When she moaned and he slid her a sideways glance, she shrugged. Pie was the best.

"So," he said. "Normally, I'd interpret that as a yes."

She sighed and he laughed.

"Yes, Declan. We have a deal."

"You want to shake on it? Seal it with a kiss?"

"Are you kidding me?"

He winked. "Just testing you."

"We're done for the day here," she said.

While he laid in a course toward what she hoped was the pier, she retrieved her race binder and put a large check in the box next to *practice new sailing skills* and *nominate a charity*. Then she added a new box for *makeover lessons*. Next to her, Declan laughed. She ignored him. It was okay to be a work in progress.

And sure, the sun would go supernova and it would take a billion years before she actually *finished* working on herself, but still. She was doing that work and her interest in Declan extended no further than the man's impressive sailing skills. She couldn't possibly be interested in anything more. He was a movie star. A professional racer and seeker after adrenaline. And while she fully planned on taking advantage of his racing expertise to cross that finish line first, she was not going to get involved with a shameless charmer.

Never ever again.

Four

Two words had governed Declan's life since the day he'd had to weigh the potential dangers of jumping off a roof with the adrenaline rush of completing a difficult stunt.

Risk.

And *reward.*

Declan had earned his place in Hollywood through hard work, sheer determination and an uncanny ability to judge that risk against its potential payoff. Those efforts had yielded a fortune, star status and now the chance to seal the deal of a lifetime. He might have been adopted rather than born into the Masterson family, but he'd prove that he had what it took to be one of them by passing this last test.

The five-thousand square foot brown-shingled mansion he temporarily called home in Martha's Vineyard was worthy of any New England blue blood family. The

interior decorator had chosen a rustic, industrial farm-
house look, both trendy and expensive, and the Atlantic was clearly visible through wide-open French doors.
The rolling, green lawns were painstakingly manicured
to perfection, billows of hydrangeas and wild grasses
surrounding the pool and the cabana. It was all perfectly
pleasant, well insulated from the ever-present paparazzi,
endlessly serene…and he itched to be anywhere else.
He had more than enough money to rent the exclusive
compound for the entire summer, or to buy it outright,
but it wasn't enough.

Nothing ever was.

Yacht races and heli-skiing, kayaking in the Arctic
and cave diving in the Great Blue Hole—none of it held
his attention for long.

In the forty-eight hours since his deal with Charlotte,
he'd brought in stylists, aestheticians and a walking
coach. The makeover team bustled around the far end
of the room, waiting for today's reluctant star. Charlotte Palsgrave had been determined to get her pretty,
spoiled way about who they sponsored for the charity
race. And as the reclusive, quiet daughter of one of the
island's oldest families, Princess got what she wanted.

Still, she'd agreed to pay his price. He'd give her that,
and when she got the million-dollar check for her beloved children's charity, he'd get the family company.
For now all he had was the steady beat of the sun on the
water, the wind that had already whipped tiny whitecaps onto the otherwise calm surface. So much peace
and quiet. Ridiculously, he still felt like that eight-year-
old boy, swept from a California foster home into a life
he could never have imagined. He'd been a miscue in
the smooth Masterson script, a wrong line, the out-of-

place story beat. Taking control of the family company would solve all that.

He'd always been hyperaware of his surroundings, a requirement of his rough childhood, so he was the first to notice the newcomer hovering in the doorway. *Gotcha*, he thought. Charlotte had agreed to come and she was the kind of person who believed a promised made was a promise kept.

At twenty-nine, she was four years younger than him, but she'd grown up in a completely different world. She was a genuine "good girl," quiet and reserved, the daughter of a New England family with deep-rooted connections to the island and a long pedigree he couldn't have cared less about. Taller than average for a woman, even in ballet flats, her brown hair was pulled back in her usual casual ponytail that ended just below her shoulders—which he knew because she toyed with the ends of her hair as she surveyed the room, watching from the sidelines as always. The perfect care with which she approached everything only made him think of messing her up, undoing all that prim tidiness.

She hesitated, clearly unsure what her next step should be. Nothing about her outfit of black yoga pants and a Martha's Kids windbreaker screamed "look at me." She'd be eaten alive in his world, so there was no reason to draw her into this game. If he'd been a better or a nicer man, he'd have allowed her to continue hiding in the shadows she liked so much. He wouldn't drag her front and center in J.J.'s game.

But since being nice wouldn't win the race and J.J.'s challenge, he sprang into action and took the decision out of her hands by striding toward her.

She registered his approach with wary caution. "Declan."

"Princess." He braceleted her wrist with his fingers, tugging her gently forward.

She grimaced. "That's not my name, Hollywood."

"Queenie," he offered. "Buttercup. Dream Girl."

"If I push you overboard after we cross the finish line, no one will blame me."

He grinned at her, delighted. "*Everyone* will blame you. I'm deeply beloved."

This made her groan. "Clearly this *everyone* hasn't heard you go off script."

He ignored the truth of her words. "A new you awaits."

This earned him another groan. "Explain to me how this helps us win the race."

Feminine and warm, the smooth tones of her voice made him think of sliding between the sheets with her, an off-limits activity as he was reformed, at least publicly. And while parading a genuine New England princess around on his arm could only bolster his good-guy image, she didn't like him. She was refined, classy and entirely, completely unimpulsive.

He was her polar opposite.

He captured her hands between his, feeling his mouth curving upward into a grin. They might be opposites at heart, but playing with Charlotte was a definite perk. Despite the princessy, uptight attitude, the woman herself was a delightful surprise package. Beneath her practical clothes she had a sweet, curvy body and legs for days thanks to her above-average height.

He hadn't dated anyone since his disastrous joke of a marriage proposal. Despite myriad opportunities, he'd been strangely reluctant. Casual sex, no matter how adventurous, was somehow no longer enough. The smile faded from his face. He had no intention of changing— only of winning.

"You could trust me," he suggested softly, startling himself.

Brown eyes narrowed. "Not a chance."

Her voice held a definite snap and not a hint of her usual politeness. He wondered if that defensiveness was due to her fiancé—but what man couldn't see the quiet beauty and wry wit she tried so hard to hide?

She tugged against his grip. "Explain the plan to me."

"Winning."

Letting go of her, he set a palm on the small of her back and steered her toward the army of people gathered around racks of clothes and a portable beauty station. As a stylist started pulling a handful of looks, Charlotte shot him a mutinous glare.

She fingered a cashmere sweater. "None of this says 'Martha's Kids.' Who pays for these?"

"I do," he said. "It's a business expense. Think of it as advertising. This is a charity race with social events and networking. Yoga pants aren't the look to go for at the gala ball. If you want people to back you, you need to sell them first."

"This is revenge."

"Really?"

She groaned. "Of course it is. You're not only stuck with me, but you can't give ridiculous amounts of money to a save-the-guinea-pigs rescue foundation."

He bit back a grin. "Most women would be thrilled."

This earned him a sideways look. "So I'm not most women."

That was true.

She said the words lightly, as if it were no big deal. He knew that forced lightness. He'd acted the role too many times himself to not recognize it. Someone had made her feel that different was bad, when in fact it was everything. Perhaps not everything was perfect in her kingdom after all. Before he could give in to the unfamiliar urge to deviate from his game plan—where he turned her into the perfect, public answer to J.J.'s demand that he act exactly like a Masterson—he shooed her toward the room designated as a temporary dressing room.

Nice was a weakness he couldn't afford when he was so close to the finish line.

Ten minutes later, when she still hadn't emerged, he rapped sharply on the closed door. It wasn't, he told himself, that he was eager to hear—and see—what she thought of the new clothes. He was busy and she was a step in his game plan, so the sooner she got on board, the sooner he could wrap this up.

"Come on out, Princess."

The answering rustle on the other side of the door had him thinking of clothes sliding over bare skin.

"My name is not Princess." Her voice radiated irritation as she tugged the door open to frown at him.

Leaning against the frame, he took her in. Dressed-up Charlotte was stunning. White linen pants clung snugly to her hips before flaring down to her ankles and a cropped, black button-up sweater bared a teasing glimpse of her stomach.

"I like this on you." He made a spinning motion with his fingers, laughing at her little growl of frustration.

"This sweater shrank in the wash." She tried to tug the edge of the sweater down and he gently caught her hands with his, his fingertips brushing bare skin. Heat flared through him.

Doing his best to ignore it, he carefully shifted her to one side and then reached around her to rummage through the rack of clothing by the door. She looked amazing, but he didn't want her to feel uncomfortable so he pulled out a white cashmere sweater with brown stripes and a Hermès scarf.

Her own clothes sat neatly folded on the bed, a T-shirt with cheery pink cartoon fish topping the pile.

"Try your shirt," he said. "With mine."

"Are you a stylist now?"

He turned around ostentatiously. "Take. Your. Shirt. Off."

He dangled the T-shirt from his hand and she moved closer to snatch it. He did his best not to notice the almost brush of her body against his, the warmth of her skin and the subtle feminine scent. Instead he studied the closed door as she shimmied out of the cropped sweater and back into her T-shirt.

"Safe?"

"Enough," she muttered.

He turned back around. She stood there awkwardly, hands fluttering at her sides as if she wasn't quite sure what to do with them. He had some ideas, but he kept them to himself and settled instead for tying the hem of her shirt up into a jaunty knot that stopped at her waist without baring any skin and then holding the new sweater out for her to slip into.

Unexpectedly, part of him wished he was doing this for someone special like a wife, someone he just had to spoil because she was his person and he needed to show her just how special she was in his eyes. That part of him was tired of the Hollywood games. It was one reason why he wanted Masterson Entertainment to be his; finally, he'd be making movies that reflected his vision rather than someone else's. It also meant he'd have a place, a chance to build on the Masterson legacy. He'd belong, once and for all.

The woman standing stiffly in front of him belonged here, in Martha's Vineyard, and most definitely here in the yacht club with its reserved, refined air. Her brisk, no-nonsense walk was endearing in its directness. She set her course and she stuck to it. She'd been all those things in yoga pants; the expensive new clothes couldn't change who she was fundamentally, but they showcased it, like a frame around a picture.

She looked curvy but strong. Tall. Not the kind of female lead he usually played opposite, who was lean and toned, telegraphing sex appeal and a body confidence that announced she knew her worth. Instead, she was more like a treasure chest or a nesting doll—so much hid beneath Charlotte's soft, calm surface.

He got the hell out of the room, leaving her to neatly fold and put away the discarded clothing. He was already sprawled on the enormous sofa when she came back out, but as soon as she stepped into the room, he barked a command to the small army of stylists who descended on her.

She's not for you.

Charlotte had many nightmares, not all limited to nighttime hours: Walking naked into a crowded room. Her teeth falling out like a bad cartoon character. Not being able to replace the money her ex-fiancé had stolen before the theft became public knowledge and her kids lost their magical summer forever because of her bad judgment. Prior to yesterday's makeover session, however, that list had not included pretty clothes, makeup or walking from point A to point B. Her afternoon at Declan's summer mansion yesterday had revealed just how unprepared she was for a life of Hollywood glam.

And as if the time he'd spent transforming her into a very expensive fashion model wasn't awkward enough, he'd added walking lessons. Posing lessons. She had actual homework to stare at herself in the mirror and practice smiling. On *top* of their sailing practice and race prep.

She'd never so much as paddled a kayak since that disastrous day when she'd come closer to drowning than she cared to remember. It still took the better part of her courage—and preferably the world's biggest life jacket rather than the sleek, non-inflatable PFD Declan preferred—to walk down the dock and get into the keelboat. Declan hadn't said anything, but he had to be disappointed. For all his flaws—and he had many—he was an international caliber sailor.

Trying to get out of bed revealed another shortcoming. Sailing used a disturbing number of muscles she hadn't known she had and she was sore. Since she'd been adamant that she needed to sail and not just sit about decoratively, Declan had reviewed basic sail positions and adjusting for "maximum wind contact."

Her attempts at sail adjustment had left them both soaked by the ocean spray she'd somehow directed straight into the boat. He'd only laughed. She'd like to think that the patience and good humor in his hazel eyes were genuine, but charm was an illusion.

What if she couldn't do it? What if he got fed up with

her ignorance and demanded a new partner? He was a Hollywood star and the biggest name participating in the race, so his wishes would be catered to. She groaned. The makeover silliness might be the smallest concession she'd be willing to grant. For Martha's Kids, she'd do almost anything. Not that she'd hop into bed with Declan or try to seduce him into a better mood—she had limits and, frankly, she doubted that sort of strategy worked outside the pages of a book. Plus the man could hardly be hurting for companionship. He was gorgeous.

Her body humming with some very pleasant recollections of just how good-looking her partner was, she finally rolled painfully out of bed and staggered over to the window. Charlotte lived in a guesthouse behind her father's house for a very modest amount of rent. A place of her own would have been great, but her salary as the director of a children's nonprofit was hardly a match for the often exorbitant rent in Martha's Vineyard. She knew she should be grateful for his assistance and most days she was. She loved being able to live here on the island year-round and her father didn't mean to make her feel less than adequate.

She had no idea why her racing partner believed she was a rich girl with unlimited access to the Bank of Dad. Hah. That couldn't have been further from the truth. She worked hard and handouts were on her Over-my-Dead-Body list. Too bad, then, that George hadn't felt the same way.

Declan, on the other hand, seemed as willing as she was to work for what he wanted. Thinking about him was bad because it made her want things, things she'd stupidly believed she shared with George. It was hard to remember that painful lesson about trusting too fast watching Declan. The casual power of his big body and the ease with which he moved around the boat and sent them flying across the water was simply too sexy. What would it feel like to have all that strength and interest focused on her? Despite the differences between them, she couldn't stop thinking about it.

She'd never felt this sort of heat and need for a man before. Certainly not for her ex-fiancé, a thought she set aside for later. She needed to focus on Martha's Kids. But something about Declan had some very erotic thoughts running through her head, and not just because the man was a Hollywood Prince Charming.

Stupid, sexy thoughts.

She had a date with a decidedly *un*sexy grant application and a mountain of paperwork. Declan was a distraction she couldn't afford when all her focus needed to be on her kids and saving their summer camp. This week she should've been paying the deposit on the campground. Planning s'mores and kayak routes. *I'm so sorry, kids.* Throat tight with guilt and anxiety, she turned away from the window.

It didn't matter that when he looked at her, she felt that just maybe he saw something—some*one*—worth looking at. She'd spent her life avoiding attention and now here he was, watching. Staring. *Seeing* her. And that made him dangerous in a way even his Hollywood characters weren't.

Five

The beloved up-island lunch spot of several presidents who enjoyed its chic, laid-back vibe and Modern American cuisine, Bryant Palsgrave's favorite restaurant looked like a white stone cottage tucked into an English country garden: Peaceful. Romantic, even. Normally Charlotte would have at least enjoyed the food, but time spent with her father was challenging, to say the least. She dug into her beet salad, hoping the honey-and-clementine dressing might sweeten her companion's words. Or perhaps her lettuce crunching would drown them out.

As always, their weekly father-daughter lunch had the same agenda: the many ways in which she'd failed to meet his expectations.

Despite retiring five years ago from a successful Wall Street career, her father still favored bespoke three-piece suits and powder blue Hermès ties. She presented him a new one yearly for Father's Day because he liked them and she knew better than to rock that boat. She'd kept the peace since her mother had walked out on them when she was seven. She'd thought a few times about trying to track her mother down and then she'd let the thought go. Shanna Palsgrave's own lack of attempts to contact her daughter spoke volumes.

"Tell me the next steps." He cut into the grilled salmon the server had set before him. "With Martha's Kids."

He'd already checked his watch twice and not, Charlotte knew, because he was tracking his resting heart rate or his steps for the day. She bored him and he had better things to do. "We're planning the annual summer camp."

"You should think bigger."

He made a dissatisfied gesture, his face falling into familiar, disapproving lines. He'd have preferred her to have a high-powered job in New York City, a job that would have afforded her a multi-million-dollar brownstone as well as a summer place. In his world, philanthropy followed a successful career or marriage to a man with political aspirations who could eventually invite his father-in-law to Washington, D.C., social events and the White House. Her older brother had made partner two years ago in a prestigious Boston law firm and was shopping for a Vineyard house to accommodate his own growing family. Their father was convinced he'd sit on the Supreme Court in a few years and Charlotte's more modest aspirations simply didn't register on the family's success scale. She loved peace, quiet and the chance to work with kids who needed her and to make her small difference in the world around her.

And yet her father insisted on reviewing her life plan with her each week, criticizing or dismissing her minor accomplishments because, as he said, he only wanted what was best for her and for Martha's Kids. He didn't understand her reluctance to grow the charity into a national organization hosting summer camps across the country. She hadn't told him about George's theft.

"Martha's Kids doesn't have the budget," she explained yet again through a throat tight with regret. *Which is my fault since George stole it without my noticing until it was too late.* "And our mission is to be a good neighbor and focus on our community."

"You could be so much more if you stopped thinking so small. Why limit yourself to just Martha's Vineyard and Massachusetts? There are foster kids elsewhere."

"I love my work." She murmured a quiet thank-you to the server who discreetly removed her largely untouched salad and replaced it with her entrée.

"Think larger," he snapped.

Translation: don't screw this up. She was actually just the interim director of Martha's Kids, although the board of directors had made it clear that they'd renew her two-year contract if she did well. And she'd had a shot, until George. "Still loving what I do."

That had her father explaining, his voice growing louder, about the greater possibilities for funding and scope if she took Martha's Kids national. He didn't understand there was enough work right there in Martha's Vineyard. He only saw what could be improved upon.

"Not everything has to be bigger or better," she said when he turned his attention back to his salmon. "Maybe Martha's Kids works exactly the size it is?"

She focused on her chicken while he blustered on.

She'd spent the morning stalling the program director, who wanted to know when she could start hiring camp counselors for the summer program. The answer was no time soon, although Charlotte had stopped taking her own salary to preserve their remaining funds. The program director was concerned—and not the only person who suspected something had gone badly wrong. Charlotte had to tell them soon.

A stir at the front of the restaurant had her head turning, grateful for a distraction as an outsize wave of whispers spread through the dining room. A moment later, she saw why.

Declan stood in the doorway. Her stupid breath caught because, really, the man was too sexy for her own good. From the looks the other diners sent his way, she wasn't the only one who had noticed. He followed the hostess toward the Palsgrave table with a confident stride.

"Charlotte and I have a sailing date," Declan said, when he'd reached their table.

This was news to her and most definitely not on the schedule tucked inside her race prep binder. They sailed every other day, after she finished at Martha's Kids. The alternate slots were, unfortunately, blocked off for more of Declan's "makeover lessons." She still thought they were a waste of time, but so far she'd had walking lessons, along with some highly entertaining explanations from Declan on how best to pose for the inevitable camera, where he pretended to be either a high-society lady or a successful influencer. He didn't mind laughing at himself, she'd learned.

Declan's eyes brimmed with mischief. "Let's go." He gestured toward the exit as if abandoning her father mid-salmon was perfectly reasonable.

"Declan's teaching me how to sail," she said, hoping to defuse the irritation building on her father's face. He hadn't decided yet if the apparent double-booking was simply another example of her incompetence or intentional rudeness on Declan's part.

"It will take more than an afternoon," he said. "You'd still be on the island next year. Our Charlotte's no Kate Middleton."

Ha ha. She opened her mouth to say something— she had no idea what—but Declan crossed his arms over his chest, frowning down at her father, clearly not impressed with the unfavorable comparison to English royalty. Although now that she thought about it, she wasn't at all sure that Kate had even won her last charity race. Ouch.

"Charlotte just has to be Charlotte," Declan said. "She doesn't have to be someone else to win."

Her father ignored this.

"Couldn't hold on to George Moore," he said, in that overloud, jovial voice he used when he was *just joking.* She'd never figured out if he genuinely didn't understand that his jokes hurt, or if he merely pretended ignorance. "Her fiancé," he added, in case no one in Martha's Vineyard had explained Declan's very public abandonment to him. "He ran. Bolted. Couldn't do it anymore.'

By *it,* he meant Charlotte because of course she was the problem. The dumpee was always the one who hadn't been enough.

"His loss." Declan sounded as if he actually meant it. He turned to Charlotte. "Can you finish quickly?"

She decided to live dangerously. "I'll take it with me."

Her father had a rule that you left what you didn't

eat—Palsgraves didn't do leftovers—but her chicken was amazing and she was hungry. Plus, she was the Palsgrave who lived on a budget, thanks to the sad state of her checking account. Hunger won out over pride any day. Declan caught the eye of the waiter hovering nearby and her plate was whisked away.

"We should go," she half shouted, hopping to her feet before her father could protest.

Something flashed in Declan's eyes, but he just nodded. Usually this would be where she'd start apologizing, but what could she say? "Sorry that my dad's such an ass"? Plus, she almost thought she was done with that sort of thing: apology things. She tested the thought and realized she wasn't feeling as stressed as she usually would. She felt—okay. Even a little bit happy.

An amused smile played about the corners of Declan's handsome mouth. He saw far more than he let on, and if her father thought he was just a handsome face he was mistaken, even if the odds of his admitting to being less than perfect were low. So instead of wishing for the impossible, she savored the short walk out of the restaurant and the way Declan's hand rested on the small of her back. The gesture was old-fashioned, but she liked the small connection. It told her that he was there with her. For the few moments it took them to walk outside, she let herself enjoy the sensation of someone having her back.

"I won't screw this up," she told him. "I won't lose the race for us."

A luxury sports car waited out front, black, low-slung and expensive. He opened the passenger door for her, tipped the valet as she slid inside, and then went around and got into the driver's seat.

He gave her a look that she couldn't interpret. "This entire race isn't on you, Charlotte."

He put the car into gear with an easy confidence.

"Did I miss something? Am I a good sailor suddenly?"

"You try hard." His voice was rough and low, a sexy rasp that made her think about suggesting they forget about sailing lessons and races. The man gave her goose bumps.

"Trying isn't enough." True story.

"It is for me." He paused. "Tell me something. Would you kick me out of the boat if I made a mistake?"

"Of course not," she said. "But we both know you're not going to do that."

"I make plenty of mistakes."

She shrugged and focused her attention out the window. Martha's Vineyard in the summer was beautiful. "I'm the novice sailor. You're the one who's going to win this race."

Faster than she would have liked, he was pulling them into a parking spot at the marina. Not that he'd broken any speed limits—despite the obvious speed potential of his car, he was a careful driver and she'd never felt unsafe with him. She got out without waiting for him to come around and open the door, and then they set off down the dock.

Which was surrounded on three sides by water.

In truth, she would have been happier if this was a land race.

Declan shot her an assessing glance and she bared her

teeth at him, wondering if *nothing to see here* was a sentiment she should tattoo on her face.

"Do you want to finish eating first?" he asked.

"Nope." She couldn't risk throwing up in front of him. "Let's do this." She eyed the boat, which was at least a great distraction.

She could focus on whether or not the ocean was truly out to get her rather than, say, on the size and heat of Declan's large body so close to hers. She wasn't attracted to him like that. He was a big, well-built guy who was confident in his skin and who had a hidden sweet streak. That wasn't *actually* a basis for attraction.

Wait. It totally was.

She blew out a breath. The need and desire she sometimes felt around Declan didn't mean anything. There weren't any real feelings there, feelings like liking and attachment, intimacy and a commitment that extended further than beating the butts of their fellow racers. He certainly didn't care about her or even value her, while she was using him for his sailing skills. It was good that she could be so practical about all this.

"Your chariot, milady," he teased, gesturing toward the boat. "I'm at your command. Just tell me what you want."

Then he jumped down into the boat, held up his hands to help her in, and, when she insisted on doing it by herself, smiled and busied himself with casting off while she put on her life jacket and wondered if this was a case in which two jackets were better than one.

How far *was* she willing to go to secure Declan's cooperation? The makeover dare was a small price to pay when she would do almost anything short of—

Sleep with him! her body suggested gleefully. *Let's sleep with him! Take one for the team!*

It was good she had boundaries, she decided as she dropped awkwardly into the boat and he got them underway. Otherwise she might have added *sex up the movie star* to the day's checklist.

Six

Declan worked out his frustrations on the ocean, while Charlotte recorded rig tuning observations on their waterproof notepad. She liked working her way down her list and checking stuff off. And she definitely liked knowing what came next. Still, she'd let him drive her out to the marina and she'd gotten on the boat after a little teeth gritting. His favorite part had been when she'd kicked off her ballet flats and rolled up the white cotton pants that snugged her hips.

From her tight expression and the way she fidgeted with the straps on her life jacket, she hadn't magically conquered her fear of deep water yet. He debated asking if she wanted to talk about it, but the look she shot him said *that* topic was off-limits. He also considered introducing the topic of Bryant Palsgrave and grade A asshole, but he was shockingly willing to avoid talking about fathers. His own was a problem, so *glass houses* and all that.

Eventually, when he fell into an easy silence, Charlotte started barking out orders, trying to sail their boat by proxy if not by skill. Cute. He'd managed to keep a straight face while steering them out into open water. Who'd have thought he'd find his prickly, bossy race partner so much fun? But after their rather contentious start, she'd been a good sport about her makeover. And from the stack of beginner sailing books he'd spotted in her tote bag yesterday, she'd tried to learn the basics of sailing.

Not that it mattered because he knew enough about sailing for the both of them. Their two-person keelboat might be smaller and far simpler than the monohulls he'd raced in the world's most exotic locations, but the principles remained the same. On the water was the one place he'd always felt at home—as if he belonged and had nothing to prove.

And after Charlotte had practiced her new sailing skills, he'd taken over, sending the boat flying over the water. For the next two hours he'd switched between running the boat on upwind and downwind legs to get a feel for how she went. The more time they spent on the water, the better race day would go.

Charlotte was a good sport. Other than the ocean itself, nothing seemed to bother her: Not the water that constantly splashed them. Not the salt spray that turned her sleek ponytail into something wilder and larger. Not the sun that was slowly turning her cheeks pink. She moved where he directed, adjusting their placement in the boat to respond to the wind angles.

He'd expected his uptown girl to hate the glorious

messiness of sailing. But maybe there was a whole lot more to her than he'd first thought. Maybe she was more than daddy's princess, the rule-following good girl who'd gone from sitting on the volunteer board of a children's charity to stepping in to run the entire organization when the previous director had retired unexpectedly. He knew he wasn't being entirely fair to her. She was a person with many sides, not a cookie cutter, one-dimensional woman.

He watched her from his side of the boat, taking in her quiet enjoyment as she pointed to a pair of seabirds winging past overhead. He couldn't help comparing this smiling, relaxed Charlotte with the contained woman he'd surprised at lunch. His mind replayed those moments—the disapproving looks her father had aimed at Charlotte, at him, at the world.

A short internet search last night had uncovered some mentions of Charlotte's engagement and subsequent un-engagement. Most of it focused on her now ex-fiancé, a man who'd never met a camera he didn't like. It was hard to imagine the reserved Charlotte with such a man, but he'd be the first to admit that photographs couldn't capture everything. It certainly went a long way toward explaining Charlotte's reluctance to put herself forward and made him want to show her what he'd started to see: that she was smart, loyal and had her heart in the right place. Anyone who didn't value those qualities was a fool.

The real question was, why did Declan want to make it up to Charlotte? Why did he care if she'd been hurt?

He was turning that thought over in his head when Charlotte grabbed for a loose line.

"Charlotte," he said in a warning tone. She didn't

listen, probably because she did things for herself even when she wasn't sure what she was doing. She pulled on the tail of the line and of course it climbed right up the mast, as lines did.

"Wow." She tilted her head back and squinted up at the halyard. "That was not part of the plan."

He gave her a small smile. "Didn't think it was."

She sighed. "Tell me how I fix this."

Now it was his turn to sigh. "Maybe you let me fix it."

She shook her head. "My mistake. My responsibility."

He adjusted the sails, slowing the boat. "A quick pit stop and we're good."

Moving lightly on his feet, he moved up to the bow and dropped the anchor and chain, then let the chain pay out. The boat swung in a lazy arc, coming about as it slowed to a stop.

She watched him, suspicion all over her pretty face. "Are we stuck here? Because I have to go to work tomorrow, so this doesn't work for me."

"I'll always get you home, Charlotte." He toed off his shoes, following her eyes as they stared at his bare feet. "Ask nicely and I'll give you a strip show."

She rolled her eyes. "What are you really doing?"

He looked at her calmly. "Getting our halyard back."

"You're going up there? I'm sure I can figure this out." She looked at the top of the mast as if it were Everest.

"You don't need to worry about me." She worried about everyone else, as far as he could tell, so adding one more person to that equation was unnecessary.

"Really?" Her voice rose, concerned. "You're just going to climb up there and grab it? What if you fall?"

He locked eyes with her. "I won't. Promise."

The mast was maybe thirty feet. He'd climbed far higher. Hell, he'd fallen farther as a working stuntman. This was easy.

"Stop," she demanded. "I have a firm policy that no one else pays for my mistakes."

She surged to her feet, apparently determined to single-handedly prevent him from going aloft. It wasn't a big boat and Charlotte hadn't quite found her sea legs. He reached out to steady her, and the fact was, he didn't mind pulling her close. Not at all. She felt amazing even if she'd decided to punctuate her claim by stabbing him in the chest with her index finger.

More than amazing, he amended. It was embarrassing how much he liked holding her close like this.

"Charlotte." He kept his voice low. Calm. He'd figured out on day two of their partnership that Charlotte didn't like confrontation or conflict. "I've got this." He rubbed a small circle over her cheek. "So what if you let go? It's just a mistake. A small one. Okay?"

"Sure," she said, sounding uncertain. Damn it. Charlotte wasn't perfect. Fact was, she made mistakes. But so did he. A shocking number of mistakes, if he was honest, with the most recent one being the deal he'd made with J.J. to nail down his ownership of Masterson Entertainment. He'd spent years longing for his old man's recognition and appreciation, but he hadn't appreciated the freedom of not wanting those things. Winning this race had seemed like an easy way to seal his deal with the old man.

Mistake number one.

Mistake number two had been letting J.J. know just how badly he wanted the family company. He'd built that business for two years, developing a roster of new talent, crafting deals, taking chances on a script or two that no one else would green-light. It had just started to pay off and he had a team of guys who needed that work, who'd bet their careers on Declan making good on his promises. And it felt great to know that he had J.J. over a barrel, that the man couldn't renege on their contract as long as Declan won this stupid race. So he'd win, no matter what…

And that had led straight to mistake number three.

J.J. would think Charlotte was perfect.

He didn't like the thought of Charlotte getting drawn into J.J.'s schemes, even if she was getting something she wanted out of their deal—a whole lot of money for her charity. He hardly even registered that he had drawn her closer, gathering her up in his arms, slowly enough—or so he told himself—that she'd had plenty of time to object.

"I can't even with you," she muttered.

She didn't move away, though.

He noticed that. He noticed everything about her, which was an entirely different problem. Water slapped against the side of the boat, rocking them gently. *Very* gently. Charlotte promptly lost her balance, throwing her arms around him.

"I'm blaming you for this," she muttered.

With a head shake, he steadied her. Even through the life jacket, she felt warm and soft in his arms. Of course, she steadied him right back because Charlotte was a big believer in keeping things even.

"Is this okay?" he asked quietly.

She nodded.

"You have to say it."

"You," she whispered, then she pushed up onto her tiptoes, her mouth reaching for his. Good enough.

Her hands came up to cup his face and then she tugged him down toward her. He went willingly, wrapping his hands around her back, steadying her a second time as he braced them both. Slowly, to give her time to change her mind, he erased the space between them and kissed her. Soft. Careful. His mouth asking for something more.

She shifted back when the boat rocked, staring at his mouth, her gaze flying up to hold his. "Yes?"

"Yes."

Tucking her up against him, he kissed her again. She relaxed into him, letting her body rest against his.

"This is just to shut you up," she told him.

His own mouth curved in an answering smile. "Anything you want, Charlotte."

Turned out, what his lady wanted was *more*. She laughed and then she gasped when he kissed her deeper, nipping teasingly at her lower lip. He drank in the sweetly cautious sound, answering with a rougher, hungrier noise of his own, holding nothing back. There wasn't an inch of space between them and he liked that. Wrapping her ponytail around his hand, he lost himself in a kiss that was better than anything he'd ever felt before.

When he finally pulled back, her eyes were closed, a flush of pink on her cheeks and all of her soft and trusting. He held on to her, not ready to let go. And that led to another soft brush of his lips over hers and then *she* kissed *him*. Hot. Sweet. Letting him in more than he'd ever dreamed possible.

"Wow." She bit her lower lip when they finally pulled

back and stared at each other. "That was something. It's a good thing we got that out of our systems."

As if. He smoothed her hair back from her face. "We're not done. All you have to do is tell me what you want. Anything you want."

She took a step back and dropped down onto her seat, pulling the band out of her hair and smoothing her hair back into a neat tail. She shook her head, her words coming out less than steady. "Fix the boat, boat master."

He winked. "As my lady wishes."

Anything you want. Charlotte replayed those three dangerous words in her head as Declan did exactly as he'd promised: what she'd asked for. He went up the mast effortlessly, the muscles in his broad back bunching as he climbed. In less than five minutes, he had the AWOL line secured and was making his way back down toward the deck. And her. The way he handled things made her feel safe, the sensation unfamiliar and too tempting, and as much as she hated to admit it, he made her want *things*. Declan-shaped, sexy, forever-sized things.

He secured the line once he had his feet back on the deck and turned to look at her. "You're in the driver's seat."

She absolutely wasn't.

He met her gaze. She wasn't sure he knew how to back down. "You are. You've got this."

She didn't, but she got up to sit at the helm.

"You want to talk about it?" He sat down next to her. "Or you can knock me overboard if you'd rather. Freeze me out the way you do everyone else."

She focused on the tiller. Maybe it was the rudder?

She had no idea how people named boat parts, but the words on her list of sailing terms weren't easy to memorize. "I don't freeze people out."

"You do, but it's none of my business," he said slowly. "Not really."

She stared fiercely at a point on the horizon. "I don't have the best track record when it comes to men. I'm sure you've heard the stories by now. There are a ton, all embarrassing. I met this guy when we were both working at Martha's Kids. We dated, a real whirlwind romance, and he asked me to marry him. I said yes. We'd known each other for two months and it seemed so magical. Like a modern-day fairy tale. Here he was, my very own Prince Charming, going down on one knee and promising me forever."

Declan didn't look amused or surprised. He just nudged a line and nodded for her to keep going when it was embarrassing how much she'd already shared. "I'm not one to judge, obviously. You know the stories about my first proposal." His shoulder pressed against hers, warm and steady. "Let's just say that I did not get that right. Tell me what happened next?"

Confessing to Declan was a bad idea. The pictures of his failed proposal were everywhere and of course the locals had been interested when he'd agreed to headline the charity race. But even if he'd come off as impulsive and too playful about something she believed, deep in her heart, should be the decision of a lifetime, the actress's refusal had surprised many people. George's rejection, on the other hand, hadn't been unexpected. At all.

"He changed his mind," she said. "That's the long and

the short of it. I wasn't what he wanted. So he broke up with me and left Martha's Vineyard. The end."

"Would you want him back?" The strong, warm shoulder pressed against hers a little more firmly and his hand covered hers on the tiller. "Because someday he'll realize he's made one hell of a mistake and he'll come back."

She looked down at his hand and hers. "That won't happen. Is that what you thought would happen with you and the actress? Or is this a heads-up that you're planning your reunion?"

"No." He shook his head. "I wouldn't be here kissing you if I were waiting for her to change her mind. Sometimes mistakes are just mistakes."

She nodded. "George didn't love me and thinking that he did was my mistake. He was charming. Everyone loved him. It was all so easy. So when he walked away *so easily*, I learned a few things and I won't make that mistake again. You and I—"

"Have a race to win," he said softly. "I get that."

He had no idea just how important winning was. "I can't afford another one-way relationship. So I need to learn how to sail this stupid boat and we need to race."

"And win," he said.

"Yes. Winning is very important. I wish—" What was that saying? If wishes were horses, beggars would ride. She recognized that she was headed into dangerous territory, so she switched directions. "We'd never be a real couple. I'm the boring, quiet local girl who will stay on this island her entire life and I'm good with that."

"And who am I?" he asked, sounding curious.

"You're our Hollywood Prince Charming. A star temporarily visiting. People expect you to be with someone

like you. Your real girlfriend would be put together and
beautiful, successful and glamorous. You can't force the
pieces from two different puzzles together."

"A summer boy." He sounded unhappy.

"We come from two different worlds," she said. "Everyone knows that. And once the race is over, I'll stay
here and you'll go back. To Hollywood. To your glamorous life with the, the—"

"The other movie stars and pretty people."

He leaned over and brushed a soft kiss over her
mouth, his fingers sinking into her hair to hold her
still. And she might have gasped—just a little—in surprise but she certainly didn't want to get away from
him. The man was addictive, as was the smell of sun
and salt on his skin. Golden, warm and present—three
of her favorite adjectives—and she didn't want to let
go when he released her.

"But I'm here now," he said, voice husky.

She nodded, because the man made a good point.
She'd had a point of hers to make, she thought, floating in a sea of sensual warmth, but then he gave her
another kiss and picked her up as if she weighed nothing, settling her on his lap as his arms closed around
her. While she tried to remember why she'd wanted to
argue, he sent their boat flying over the water.

The wind pushed at them, almost tearing the breath
from her mouth even as it stung her eyes. But it felt
so good. Sailing—*racing*—had been an unwelcome
challenge, an obstacle to overcome, and the only solution she had left to fix her George-sized mistake. This,
though… This made her feel alive and had her laughing at nothing in particular.

"Who are we racing?" she yelled into the wind.

"No one," he yelled back. "Everyone. But we're totally winning."

She shook her head. The man was crazy.

"Trust me." He tugged her a little closer, which should have been impossible unless they were naked and he was—she squirmed and he groaned. And then, "Charlotte?"

"Yeah?" she whispered, knowing that somehow he'd hear her despite the wind that whipped away the sound.

"Do you trust me?"

"Enough," she said, leaning back into him. Because it was true that she felt safe with him, safe in a way she never had with anyone, and not just because she was sure he wouldn't capsize them or let her fall overboard.

His mouth brushed over her ear. "Good," he growled. "Hold that thought."

She laughed and he kept his arms around her even as he did something that made the keelboat pick up speed until they were flying over the water, racing that invisible opponent as the wind pushed them toward the harbor.

Seven

Walking the red carpet had never featured on Charlotte's bucket list. While her childhood self had played dress-up, trading shorts and T-shirts for tulle, fake diamonds and three-inch plastic heels, that had been a game. Sometimes she'd been a princess; sometimes a movie star. Once she'd crowned herself the all-powerful ruler of the universe. The real deal was exciting and addictive, frightening and overwhelmingly loud—and that was from the inside of the limo she'd shared with her father.

The ride from the Palsgrave compound to the fancy resort hosting tonight's event had been too short. Their driver pulled into the wide, circular drive, joining a line of luxury town cars and limousines. The Vineyard loved its social events. The front of the hotel had been decorated with lights and swaths of flowers. Spotlights swept the night sky and an actual red carpet led past a phalanx of reporters and then up the marble steps and inside. Cameras flashed and reporters screamed as the occupants of the car preceding theirs got out.

She'd spent her entire life hiding in plain sight and yet here she was, about to walk the red carpet into a celebrity fundraiser. At least she looked every inch the princess she'd pretended to be as a child. A stylist had sent a vintage 1920s flapper dress the color of her favorite peonies. Tier after tier of pink crystal fringe swirled around her when she moved. It was whimsical and almost like walking in ocean spray. Delicate crystal-embellished Louboutin slingback sandals and a clutch completed the outfit. She was an elegant, playful version of herself. Princess Charlotte.

Yes was a powerful word. She'd said *yes* to George when he'd proposed. *Yes* to the opportunity to crew a race boat. And *yes* to Declan's makeover plan that had upended her quiet life and sent her careening down a rabbit hole like Alice, except she'd landed smack in the middle of Declan's life—his Hollywood life—and not a topsy-turvy wonderland.

If she got out of the car, her life would never be quite the same again. She'd walk inside, holding up her end of the devil's bargain she'd made with Declan, and people would talk. They'd pay more attention than they ever had to Martha's Kids, attention that would make keeping secrets almost impossible. And while she'd always known the truth would come out, she'd wanted to fix the damage first. The limo inched slowly forward. She still had time to back out. Not much time, but enough.

The phone clutched in her hand buzzed and her father

frowned as Declan's message flashed across her lock screen. Delayed—meet you inside, Princess. You've got this.

The publicist's original plan had Declan meeting the car to walk her inside. Now, she'd be flying solo since her father wasn't doing the red carpet and would be driven to a side entrance. "Declan's been held up," she said.

Her father shook his head. "He's not really interested in you. Why would he ever choose you?" He gestured outside the window at the hotel lit up like a fairy-tale castle. Even inside the car, she could hear the muted roar of the waiting crowd, a human ocean of people coming and going, rushing in to meet the new arrivals and then chasing out after them. "You're a convenient prop, an accessory. He's a Hollywood star who dates glamorous women." When she made a noncommittal noise, he continued. "There's that sex scandal he was involved in before he came here—the man scaled a balcony naked to propose to a woman he barely knew. He'll never settle down. He'll always be hunting for the next new face. Watch. He'll have moved on by the end of the race and he'll have some movie star or famous model on his arm by then."

What her father meant, she thought, was that a woman like Charlotte couldn't hold a playboy's interest and that Declan's interest in her would fade. That was fine, she told herself. They weren't a couple—they were partners with a common goal. Partners were good. Partners were *better*.

"Perhaps I chose him," she said. Because that was a possibility, too, wasn't it? Declan had a choice, but so did she. She had to choose him, too. Her father shot her a dry look, but she ignored it. Or tried to. Some things were still a work in progress.

The car stopped and someone opened the door. The flash of cameras blinded her. Declan's lessons rushed through her head: Smile. Don't stop for questions. Don't go off script.

She got out of the car and paused as an army of men and women in discreet black suits directed the flow of celebrity traffic and corralled the photographers and curious summer tourists. An honest-to-God red carpet led toward the ballroom, but first she had to make it past the media. The click of their camera lenses sounded like a thousand cicadas chiming in at once.

She reminded herself that she liked cicadas just fine.

Funny, but her pulse still sped up, straight into heart attack territory. Mentally, she drew up a list. Step one: get out of the car. Done! Step two: shut the door. Or did she leave that for the driver? Hadn't Meghan Markle gotten in all sorts of trouble for closing her own door? Next: do a discreet check to make sure her dress wasn't caught up in her panties. Then: Take the first step. Take the next.

Repeat that last one a thousand times and she'd be inside and under cover. It was a great plan.

She managed half of one step before a minder rushed over and started hissing instructions to her. Walking—and stopping—was more complicated than Charlotte had imagined it could be. She told herself that she might not be a Hollywood princess, but that tonight she looked like one. She even had a loaner Prince Charming somewhere and it would be downright rude to keep him waiting. Fun, but rude. She grinned at *that* thought and that was the picture that would run tomorrow, her rueful, laughing, too-real smile as she fast-walked past the people waiting for her and the other stars of tonight's celebrity event. *Welcome to Declan's world*, she thought.

Declan snuck his sports car into the employee parking lot before heading into the hotel through the back entrance. The place was bustling, the event well underway. Glamorous guests dressed in expensive cocktail attire and a fortune in jewelry packed the ballroom and he spotted dozens of famous faces.

A week of pouring rain at a shoot site had forced Masterson Entertainment to rethink the final stunt sequence for a major film, a problem that had compounded when the leading stuntman had been injured and the rain had stopped unexpectedly. A replacement stuntman and fire hoses had saved the shot, but the negotiations had delayed Declan's arrival. He strode through the crowd, acknowledging greetings and looking for Charlotte.

He'd wondered if she'd balk at doing the red carpet alone and ask her driver to take her around back to skip it, but from early reports she'd done well, displaying the same quiet courage she'd shown on the water. He found her at the edge of a small group of guests, smiling politely.

Pink was the perfect color for her. Her hair had been pulled up in a sleek twist on the crown of her head, baring her neck and shoulders in lines that were as elegant and classy as the woman herself. The dress hugged her curves and showcased her long legs, strands of beads twirling out around her when she turned to greet a newcomer. He'd teased her that she was a princess, but tonight she was all queen.

The stylist had originally pulled a classic ivory sheath for her, pretty and soft, and entirely forgettable. But *he* couldn't forget her, and he wanted everyone to see Charlotte the way he saw her, a surprise no one had seen coming.

Snagging a flute of champagne from a waiter, he walked up to her, setting his hand against the small of her back and offering her the champagne.

"You shouldn't have," she said.

He grinned. "You want to make a list of all the reasons, don't you?"

She shook her head, but took the champagne. "Thanks so much."

He eased her away from the group. "How are we playing this?"

"Asking for my advice?"

"You're good at planning," he said lightly. "And we're on the same team."

"True." She cast an assessing gaze around the room. "The rules give us a one-minute head start on race day for every ten thousand dollars in donations we bring in tonight. So we can either pitch the big donors or try to hit as many groups as possible."

"Or we can bring them to us," he said, plucking the champagne flute from her and handing it to a passing waiter.

"With what? A nice hunting call? Here's a tip," she mock-whispered. "People generally run the *other* way when they're asked to hand over their money."

"With a show. Follow my lead." He wrapped his arms around her back and dipped her low. Her hands fisted in the lapels of his tuxedo jacket. She looked surprised. And unsettled. But she didn't look away from him and he couldn't stop looking at her, either, partly because she was stunning and there was nothing between his palms and the smooth, warm skin of her back. Mostly, though, because he wanted her to realize that he wanted nothing more than to peel her out of her dress and show her exactly how she made him feel.

He kissed her lightly, a brief brush of his mouth over hers, there and then gone as he righted her. Then he twirled her in a circle that sent the beads on her dress flying as he reached for her hands, bringing them to his mouth and brushing another kiss over her fingers. "Beautiful, partner."

"Thank you," she whispered, sounding as if she didn't believe him one bit.

A camera shutter clicked softly nearby. She drew a deep breath. The audience made her nervous, as if it somehow changed how he saw her, as if she had to perform to someone else's expectations. He'd meant it when he said she was beautiful.

The photographers called out their names, urging them to turn first in one direction and then another. Together. Arms around each other. Embracing. No one asked for a solo shot—their kiss had done the trick.

"That was ridiculous," she muttered.

"Window dressing," he said. "Watch. Now they'll all come to us because they're curious."

He was right. Guests walked up to them and introduced themselves, smiling and posing for the ever-present photographers. He knew the event's organizers were glad to have his name, his famous face and the movie star power—because that was the point of a fundraiser. Charity wasn't inexpensive and no foundation ever had as much money as it wanted. He liked Martha's Kids' focus on providing kids with a specific summer experience rather than vaguer, loftier goals like *promoting independence* or *developing lifelong skills*.

Charlotte turned out to be shockingly good at steering him toward various groups of guests, although he gave her credit for not just picking the ones with the deepest pockets. The newest couple was a pair of summer residents, one of the many who flocked to the Vineyard during the summer months. She was the CEO of an online yoga start-up, while he managed a hedge fund on Wall Street. Wealthy, but not recognizable celebrities, they were starstruck.

"Declan loves kids." Charlotte directed a smile at the wife's obvious baby bump. "It's why he's passionate about supporting Martha's Kids."

"Kids are great," Declan agreed. "I'm sure we can all agree on that. It's too bad, though, that not all of them have the same opportunities—and that's where Martha's Kids comes in."

Charlotte launched into a charming explanation of her foundation's summer programs and the kids they served, while the couple smiled and nodded.

"Summer camp is my happiest memory from childhood," Charlotte said.

"I was always the homesick one," the man laughed. "I pestered everyone at home constantly, asking when I could leave."

"Not me." Charlotte shook her head, making her sleek ponytail bounce. "I would have stayed forever if they'd let me."

"Did you go to summer camp growing up?" the husband asked, looking at Declan.

He slid the man a look, but it appeared to be an innocent question. "No. I was in and out of foster care when I was younger," he said. "Summer camp wasn't an option for me, but I would have loved what Martha's Kids offers. Every kid should have the chance for campfires and marshmallows, canoes and arts and crafts. Working in Hollywood, in the industry, as a stuntman was a lot harder and far less safe. You realize this when you're on your first set, at the top of a steep hill and the director's yelling for you to just ride your bike down it as if God's angels will lift you up if you crash."

"Did you?"

"Sure." He lifted one shoulder. "And one of the production assistants patched me up afterward. We got the shot, so it was a good day."

The dad-in-training looked like he might be taking notes for his future baby. "So you started as a stuntman?"

"And then transitioned into acting. Met a lot of people, learned a few things." Which was an understatement. He hadn't wanted to trade in on the Masterson name, wanting to earn his place. "I'd go into an audition in the early days, cocky and sure I had what it took, and then I'd take a good look around the room and see that casting had ordered up a dozen men who looked just like me. Twenty of us like matching roses in a bouquet, all in beat-up jeans and a white Oxford shirt. You learn fast that you're replaceable."

"But you're not replaceable," the guy pointed out.

"Not now." He pulled a face. "I had to work hard to get to that point and I'm not complaining about that. But I learned fast that, at the end of the day, the problems you face on-screen are make-believe. The real problems are what the kids whom Martha's Kids sponsors face. Homelessness, poverty, parental addiction, hunger—they're overcoming the hard stuff, which is why Charlotte and I are racing. And also because I know I'm damned lucky, like they're lucky, to have her on my team."

He winked at Charlotte, who picked up his story without missing a beat.

"Although he would have been a nightmare to keep safe." She grinned, nudging his shoulder companionably with her own. "This passion of his for climbing and stunts didn't just develop overnight. Imagine an eight-year-old Declan in one of our kayaks."

There was more laughter and then the pair shared a few summer camp hijinks of their own. Declan laughed and smiled. Then he stopped watching their companions and started watching Charlotte. She radiated a genuine and warm interest in their stories, and their audience responded to that, even if she wasn't the loudest or wittiest member of the group.

"Remember," he said when a natural break in the conversation came. "By donating tonight to the race fund, you're giving a summer camp experience to other kids—and every ten-thousand-dollar donation made to our boat specifically buys us a minute's head start on race day."

"And we'll need that extra time," Charlotte chimed in. "Because I'm better with kayaks than keelboats."

She smiled ruefully, everyone laughed, and then the couple broke out their phones and brought up the mobile giving app. They took pictures together before he and Charlotte moved toward the next group of people.

"You're good at this." He deftly swapped her warm champagne for a new, chilled glass.

"Keep thinking that," she warned him. "Because here comes trouble."

The man approaching them wasn't Declan's usual brand of trouble, either the movie kind or the paparazzi kind. He was middle-aged and wearing a tuxedo and a broad smile.

"Are you ready?" he asked.

"Always," Declan said. "But specifics would be appreciated."

"To lead off the dancing," the event host said. Charlotte merely nodded pleasantly at the man, unsurprised. His partner had been keeping secrets.

"You've been holding out on me," he said as they followed the host toward the dance floor.

Charlotte's mouth curved upward in a smile. "Consider this payback for every time you've put me on the spot."

"Right." He stared at her mouth. "Tell me what the plan is, please?"

"Can you dance, Hollywood?"

"I'm no Fred Astaire, but I can waltz. Tango. There may have been Irish line dancing on one memorable evening in Dublin."

Her smile deepened. "How about a rumba?"

"Charlotte." The woman standing opposite him laughed. "Revenge is beneath you. Be the bigger person."

"Just follow my lead, *Hollywood*."

She set her left hand on his shoulder and grabbed his right with hers. So far, so good. He hated not being able to just dive in. Hanging back was not how he'd lived his life. The music started, a Latin sound, upbeat and fast with lots of string. He slid his free arm around her back as every eye in the ballroom turned their way.

And just when he was starting to think she'd leave him standing there clueless, she whispered instructions to him. "Make a box. Two steps to the side and then one step forward. Slow, quick, quick. And, Hollywood?"

"Yeah?"

"Wiggle your hips. A lot."

Right. He scanned her face, far too aware of the tiny shifts and tensions in her body that announced her next steps. Dammit. But he loved the amusement lighting up her eyes, the smile on her face. And the bold curve of her mouth was downright beautiful, so stare-worthy that he would have missed a step if he hadn't had excellent reflexes, honed by years of performing dangerous stunts.

"Are you sure you've never done this before?"

"You're my first." He winked and what the hell… He spun her in a circle. And then another. He had no idea what he was doing. Oh, wait, he did. He was taking her up on her dare and he was winning this game.

This earned him a raised eyebrow and then she upped her game, adding spins and a sensual wiggle to her own hips that drove him wild. Desire tightened his body and had him fantasizing about stripping that dress off her and worshipping each delicious curve of her body, because it turned out that his wallflower partner who hated the spotlight could really, really dance. And when she danced with him, she forgot all about their audience. He mirrored her gestures, adding a few embellishments of his own as they danced on.

"We fit together," she said, laughing up at him.

We fit together…

She was right, he realized. Her eyes were heated, happy, as she enjoyed the moment, caught up in this thing between them. She wasn't thinking about their audience or the race. He'd have bet on that. She simply danced with him and it worked.

And losing that rightness scared him more than anything.

The music swelled and other couples joined them, turning the ballroom floor into a sea of twirling bodies. He only had eyes for Charlotte.

"You're beautiful," he said, his grip tightening on her hand as he twirled her. "But you've got to be the hardest worker I know."

Her lips parted. "Wow."

"All true."

And then the steps had them moving apart again and any more conversation wasn't happening. She beamed at him as the music ended, flushed and happy.

She grinned at him. "See? You can dance."

He pulled her up against him and grinned back. "I had an excellent teacher."

And then he lowered his head to hers and kissed her. They'd never discussed kissing, but this felt right, too. She raised up on her toes, fitting herself into his embrace, and kissed him back. She kissed like they'd danced, a slow, slow, quick that took them from an easy awareness to burning passion. A slow tease of his tongue against her closed lips was followed by the slow, teasing way she opened up for him and let him in. The quickening of their breath, the instant heat, the seductive, possessive need that raged through him... He didn't care who was watching them, not when all of him was focused on the sexy woman he held in his arms.

The applause called him back. The event host approached to congratulate them, trailing a photographer.

"That was just for our audience, right?" she asked, stepping back and putting some space between them.

He recognized the wariness in her voice and, dammit, he shouldn't have kissed her in public. She'd made it clear she wasn't dating anyone, let alone a movie star.

"It was a hell of a show," he agreed.

Except that kiss hadn't been fake.

Not completely.

Eight

Declan had stopped being impressed by wealth long ago. The Palsgrave compound overlooking the ocean barely registered. The night sky, a velvety swirl of stars and clouds, would have been worth a second look, but they weren't alone. Dammit. A photographer waited for their car in the shadows lining the driveway, camera up and ready. Good quality shots earned hundreds of dollars, but a unique picture would net thousands. Word must have got out in the hours since their "kiss."

"We have a photographer doorstepping." He kept his voice low, grateful that the windows of his luxury Mercedes were tinted. "He's waiting for you to come home, hoping to snap us together."

The possibility of a romance between him and Charlotte would have paparazzi bombarding the house. He pulled out his phone and fired off a text to his security service. Charlotte would need protection.

She shrugged. "I'm not that interesting."

He hated her easy dismissal of her own worth. "You are to me."

She pulled her evening wrap around her and picked up her clutch, not waiting for him to charge to the rescue. "Is that the new movie star math? If I'm interesting to you, then I'm interesting to your fan club out there?"

"Something like that," he said. "We need to get inside, Charlotte."

She rolled her eyes. "Since I'm not happy about the prospect of living in your car forever, yes. I do."

Before he could point out that they were partners and it was therefore a question of *we do*, she opened the door. Cameras went off in a blinding flash of light. Charlotte froze, but he was already on it, striding around the car to slam her door shut even as he put himself between her and the paparazzi.

"Come on." He squeezed her fingers gently. *Work with me.* "Let me walk you inside."

The photographers were calling her name now, demanding she look their way. There were two others he hadn't spotted, in the shadows where the security lights didn't reach. They must have parked on the main road and then walked in.

"Charlotte, are you dating Declan?"

"Is there an engagement between you?"

"Are you moving to Los Angeles?"

"Does your former fiancé know you're having an affair with a movie star? Is that why he broke it off?"

"Will you resign from Martha's Kids?"

"When's the baby due?"

"Are you kidding me?" She whirled, clearly intending

to set their unwanted company straight, but the first rule he'd learned in Hollywood was *never engage.*

Pulling her into his side, he brushed her ear with his mouth. "Front door or back? What's the fastest way in?"

She gaped and he bit back a curse. She wouldn't like these pictures. The crunch of gravel behind them announced new arrivals. They needed to move.

"You got your shot, man," he said to the nearest photographer, then tugged Charlotte up the front steps, taking her bag from her and fishing out a key. He held it up for her to see. "Yeah?"

She nodded, he got the key in the door, and then they were in. Frankly he'd expected Bryant Palsgrave to have a butler. The man seemed like the type, an impression borne out by the ostentatious entryway. A mahogany staircase with an elaborate wrought iron balustrade swept upward to the second floor. There was marble tile and more marble on the walls. An antique console held a lavish arrangement of white roses and expensively furnished rooms were visible through an archway.

Beside him, Charlotte muttered a curse of her own. Which, for the record, he hadn't heard her do, even after his showboating at the charity event. "How could they say those things?"

"It's their job. They're fishing for a reaction because reactions sell. You in a pretty dress?" He shrugged. "They snapped that at the charity event. Now they're looking for me stripping you out of the dress or a kiss. Something that will make people look."

"So they make up a baby? And a ring?"

"Yeah," he said. Did it make sense? No.

It didn't have to.

He stood there longer than he should have, trying to not think about those things. With Charlotte of all people.

She wasn't for him.

He wasn't the kind of man who did forever and he certainly hadn't seen any examples of what a good marriage might look like. J.J. had already been divorced when he'd adopted Declan and Nash and he'd never remarried.

Declan's own parents had split up before Declan's birth and Nash had a different father. He'd grown up poor and then he'd worked like hell for his place with the Mastersons. A fancy house like this one?

He didn't belong.

Which didn't stop him from remembering how that angry, resentful eight-year-old boy had felt when he'd been swept away from the latest in a long series of foster homes and dropped into J.J. Masterson's Malibu mansion. He'd worked hard to earn a place there and he'd succeeded. Almost.

Good times. Even now, years later, he still had plenty of resentment, resentment that made him restless and eager to get the hell out of Bryant Palsgrave's stifling mansion and back to his own home in the Santa Monica Mountains. He breathed better outdoors and Hollywood was a short drive away by California standards.

Charlotte shifted and he looked at her. Right. It wasn't her fault that her father was a pretentious ass and it was *definitely* Declan's fault that she was now trapped in her own home by paparazzi.

"Away from the windows." He nudged her gently.

She snorted but started walking. "This isn't one of your movies. Girls like me don't go out with guys like you."

"What's wrong with me?" He'd bet she had a list.

A long, rank-ordered list.

He followed her into a palatial living room with massive wood beam ceilings and a sea of white furniture. A sheepskin rug had been layered over a vintage Persian rug in front of a brick fireplace and French doors looked out onto a pool, a manicured expanse of lawn and the Atlantic Ocean. It was hard to imagine anyone actually sitting in here. It looked like a movie set, something he was an expert on.

Charlotte sank down onto the closest sofa and tugged off her heels with a groan. "You're so Hollywood. And I'm not."

That wasn't a bad thing. Sinking down onto his haunches before her, he rocked back onto his heels and caught her foot in his hand, then rubbed the arch. "You've got a chip on your shoulder about the whole movie star thing, don't you? There's no reason why we couldn't be together." So what if they came from different backgrounds? And so what if he had a high-profile job while she stuck firmly to behind-the-scenes work?

"If we're talking about sex," he continued. "Because that's just fun and not a fairy tale or a country song. I wouldn't fit into your pretty life here either, not for long."

She sighed and collapsed backward on the sofa. "Is that what you think? That sex is just fun?"

He tugged gently on her big toe. "If you haven't been having fun in bed, there's your problem."

This earned him a glare. "I can have fun."

Not exactly what he'd said, but okay.

He switched to her other foot. "We should talk more

about how fun sex is because right now, all those photographers outside think we're having sex."

She groaned. "We're going to have to disappoint your fan club. No baby, no engagement, no public sex."

He grinned. "So just sex in private? Because I feel the need to point out that we seem to be totally alone right now."

She tugged her foot free and stood up. "Opportunist much?"

He wasn't much of a gentleman, but he got to his feet, because she was in a dress and…she deserved all of his respect. "They'll keep trying to find a romance between us. It's a good story. They'll run with it."

"It's both ridiculous and untrue."

"It's good press," he countered. "We'll get plenty of positive coverage. Donors like happy love stories."

J.J. would like it, too, as long as Declan kept things G-rated and stuck to the fairy-tale script. A Hollywood movie star who raised money for children and fell in love with an unassuming local girl? That was story gold, and he hated that he recognized that truth even if he had no intention of acting on it. He wasn't that much of a bastard.

"We're not pretending to be in love to hoodwink people into supporting us."

"Let them take their photos and speculate that we're a real couple," he argued. "We don't confirm or deny. Eventually, they'll lose interest."

"When I'm dumped for the second time," she pointed out. "Still not seeing how this is a win for me."

"Just for a little while."

"Nope," she said. "No, not a chance. Been there, done that, didn't even get a lousy T-shirt."

"Well if all it takes is a T-shirt," he said, "that can be arranged."

She had to kill him. Bury his big, beautiful body somewhere no one would ever find him. *The movie star? Nope. Got no idea where he went.* Ugh.

She strode over to the French doors trying not to think about what he'd suggested—either the sex or the fake relationship.

"Right," he said, following her. "We can try to find some other way to sort this out, but they'll run the kiss from tonight's event, plus what they snapped outside your place. I took you home and they'll fill in the blanks after that."

The entire Vineyard would be convinced that she'd fallen in love with another handsome guy. Half the locals would plan her fairy-tale wedding, while the other half would predict she'd crash and burn.

Again.

Just months ago she'd been sure George was her person and he'd taught her a very public lesson about trusting too fast. Ever since, she'd tried to fix the destruction he'd left behind him because she was the only one who deserved to get hurt. She wasn't proud of keeping silent about all the ways he'd betrayed her, but the district attorney had asked her to keep silent while they investigated. Plus, it didn't make her a person she was proud to be and that was the truth.

She wanted to tell Declan to leave now—to walk away from her and Martha's Vineyard. But that would mean abandoning the charity boat race. Losing her chance to make Martha's Kids whole. Being dumped publicly a second time because of course she and Declan couldn't possibly be a real couple. They'd list the ways she'd been lacking. Even now she couldn't think about George without a deep, sickening feeling of humiliation. She did *not* want to do that again, but—

The bastard sensed her weakening because he said, "We can't go back in time, sweetheart, but this can work to our advantage. It won't be all bad. We'll race and then we'll go our separate ways. Things will calm down."

"Have you really thought this through? Because while you'll get to put an entire country between yourself and the breakup, I'm the one who has to stay here and explain to people I see every day. It will be very, very bad."

"We don't have to break up publicly. We can just— drift."

She snorted. *Was he delirious?*

"Think about it," he suggested. "For now, let me walk you back to your place. You're in the guesthouse, right?"

"What do you think is going to happen to me?"

He met her eyes with a level gaze. "The paparazzi could scale the wall. They could find some way in before my team gets here."

"I don't need a babysitter or a bodyguard."

"I know you think that," he said calmly. "But I have more experience with this lifestyle and I want your life to change as little as possible. My team is discreet. They'll stay out of sight unless someone gets in your face."

Lovely. Now she felt ungrateful. And yet… "This wouldn't have happened if you hadn't decided I needed a makeover. And then kissed me. In public."

"It would have happened. Because I've never met anyone like you and the degree of attraction between us isn't something I know how to manage. You're gorgeous. I want to put my hands all over you, and sooner or later, someone would have caught me doing exactly that."

Charlotte stared at him, speechless as he opened the door for her. That wasn't her usual end-of-date conversation. She replayed it in her head as she stepped through the door and headed for the guesthouse tucked between the main house and the ocean. Surrounded by boxwoods in antiqued urns, billowing pampas grass and lavender, the dark rectangle of the pool reflected back the lights of the house.

She made a shooing motion with her fingers. "You can go. White knight rescue duty done for tonight."

He grinned. "You don't want to kiss me good night? Or tell me that was a great speech?"

She sighed. "I thought the whole point was to make the stories go away?"

"This is a photographer-free zone," he said. "It could be our last chance."

The man had a point, but she didn't want to kiss him. Much. Plus didn't photographers have long-range lenses and sniper-worthy covert hiding skills? Years ago she'd toured Althorp House in England. An excited guide had recounted the grand romance between nineteen-year-old Lady Di and the Prince of Wales, noting that the room with the piano had been the only one the photographers couldn't see into. Lady Diana Spencer had spent a lot of time there. It had seemed unbearably sad to know that an entire estate was outside the door but she was trapped in a single room.

Declan put a finger beneath her chin, nudging it up. "So are we good?"

"Absolutely," she lied.

He frowned. "We're not."

"So fix it," she challenged. "If you think there's a problem."

He studied her for a moment. "There's definitely a problem. You think I only want to kiss you because everyone thinks we're in a relationship."

"Yes!"

No. She bumped her forehead against his warm, muscled chest. The real problem was that she'd already used up her mistake allowance for the year—possibly the century. Declan was nothing but risk, a charming, bad boy actor even if he was turning out to be unexpectedly thoughtful. They'd race in a week and then part ways. She wouldn't see him again, not this all-too-real man who looked at her with concern on his gorgeous face.

"So I like the way you kiss. Sue me."

He gave her a heated look, laughed…and didn't kiss her. "I've got an idea. Maybe you don't guess what I want. Maybe I tell you."

There was a serious note in his voice that she hadn't heard before.

"What would you tell me?"

Wrapping a hand around the back of her neck, he tucked her against his larger body. Her arms went around his back. He felt so good. Safe. He felt like everything she'd been missing.

"Might be easier to show you," he said roughly. A new, delicious kind of silence stretched out between them. This was the last moment of *before* because, whatever came next, things would change. For better, for worse. For pleasure.

His head lowered toward hers. "Please?"

She nodded. "Yes."

And then he erased the very small space between them and kissed her. Gently. Slowly. As if he wanted this to last for so much longer than a kiss ever could.

She kissed him back, moaning when he deepened their kiss. He made a rough sound, his fingers sliding into her hair. They kissed until they had to break apart for air. She sucked in one breath, then a second, staring at him, wide-eyed.

His own gaze was heated and far from calm. "Christ, you make me want."

"Declan," she whispered, the sound swallowed up by his mouth as he kissed her again.

Guilt and panic flooded her because it was one thing to race with this man, to fight and to sail with him. She could even let him dress her up and dance her around the floor at a Vineyard social event. Those things were easy. It was entirely different to kiss at her front door, to feel as if for this handful of moments he saw her and no one else. This was too real. Too much.

She'd rushed into a relationship too fast with George. Maybe if she'd gone slower, insisted that they take their time, she'd have seen the truth. Sooner. Maybe even from the beginning. George hadn't loved her and she— well, she'd loved the *idea* of him more than the man.

But then she wasn't thinking because Declan braced an arm by her head, leaned in and kissed her more, and her brain stopped functioning. She could only feel. *Oh, God.* He made her feel so much. His mouth, his big body pressed up against hers, the addictive warmth of him…

At some point they must have come up for air again because she opened her eyes and Declan was leaning into her, one arm still caging her in place, one hand cupping her face. His thumb stroked her cheek. He tasted like ocean, outdoors and male, and he made her want things. She was off-kilter, off-balance.

Freaking out.

She couldn't do this again. Handsome Prince Charmings didn't fall for the plain-Jane wallflowers—they faked it to conceal an ulterior agenda.

"There aren't any photographers here," she said, then ducked under his arm. "There's no need to pretend."

"You really think that was fake?"

She sighed. "You and me… We're a bad idea. Even if you kiss like a god and I really like it."

Like you.

"But?" His eyes narrowed.

"But I can't do this. I can't be someone I'm not."

He tugged her back. "I don't need you to be different."

"Makeover?" she prompted.

"That was a game," he growled. "Icing on a cupcake."

His words were lovely, even if she wasn't sure that she could believe them. Did she have a trust problem? Yes, yes she did.

He didn't look away. "I'm not George."

She opened her door. "I know that."

"And you're not Jessie," he said gently.

"So?"

"We're Declan and Charlotte."

She really, really needed to go. "I'm not ready for that," she said and went inside and closed the door behind her.

Nine

Charlotte still wasn't ready the next morning. Thanks to Declan's stylist, she had a brand-new, luxury wardrobe of sustainable cashmere and strict orders to never, ever leave the house in yoga pants again. The stylist had left a tag on one item and Charlotte had just about hyperventilated. Even if brands donated their clothing in exchange for the publicity, she directed a nonprofit and those were crazy prices.

As she came around the house, she mentally reviewed her Saturday to-do list. With the addition of the race events and practices to her usual work week, she was behind. And with no coffee or coffee creamer left in her kitchen, she had zero chance of catching up, so she was a woman on a mission when a man stepped away from the side of the house and blocked her path.

"Ms. Palsgrave." He followed this with a tip of his

chin. He wore a dark suit and tie, and although his size put him in lumberjack or football territory, he also seemed qualified to be a club bouncer or a former SEAL.

She smiled her most reliable, I'm-a-trustworthy-person smile at him. "Are you a court bailiff? Because if you are, I already shared everything I know with the district attorney."

"Not what this is about." The man's professional expression didn't waver. "Mr. Masterson sent me."

She stared at him.

"I'm security, Ms. Palsgrave. I'm Ryan."

"I really don't need a bodyguard."

He fell into step beside her. "Have you been out front this morning?"

"What's going on?" When she stopped, he stopped with her.

"Mr. Masterson said he explained that in light of the paparazzi already outside your house last night, he expected there to be more this morning."

She eyeballed her new companion suspiciously. "Was he right, Ryan? One-hundred-percent, no asterisks right? Because if so, I have complaints."

This earned her a bark of laughter from Ryan. "He usually is, ma'am. I'd like to review the situation with you and run some options if you intend to leave the property today."

"Ryan." She waved her empty travel mug at him. "I'm not a prisoner in my own house. All I want is coffee. I promise that I am supremely boring and anyone who is out there will lose interest fast."

Ryan tapped his phone screen and brought up a series of photos from in front of the house. She counted one, two, six—no, make that *seven* guys in jeans and T-shirts with expensive-looking camera gear. They were all staring at the front door with far more interest than it merited.

"Coffee," she said. "It's what makes the world go round."

Okay. So it was really the trifecta of coffee, chocolate and doughnuts, but a man with Ryan's build probably didn't acknowledge the existence of sugar.

Ryan tapped something into his phone and hers buzzed.

What kind of coffee do you want? Declan asked.

She ignored the warmth spreading through her and concentrated on her righteous indignation. "Did you tattle on me?"

"My job is to keep you safe."

Uh-huh. Because she was just surrounded by vicious predators. And also because she was a delicate flower who needed protection. Since that wasn't a battle she could win, she settled for tormenting her celebrity faux boyfriend. A good man would know how his girlfriend takes her coffee.

The text she received back said, I can buy one of everything, but then it'll take twice as long. Ryan says you're desperate and to come and save him.

As if. She snorted, eying her new nemesis, who hadn't budged from where he blocked her easy access to the outside world.

"You should let him bring you coffee," Ryan said. "Mr. Masterson has done this before. He knows how to handle the press."

"*Mr. Masterson* got caught scaling a balcony in his boxer briefs. How does that make him an expert?"

Ryan shrugged. "It makes him an expert on what not to do. And I wasn't working that night."

Right. "Were you working last night?"

"No, ma'am."

"What kind of coffee do you want then?"

After Ryan had been convinced to place a coffee order, she texted Declan back with their requests. She wasn't stupid enough to turn down free caffeine delivery, even if she was stupid enough to kiss the man in a very public place.

She received another text that announced, Be there in ten.

And then, proving once again that Declan had mind-reading powers, he sent a picture. Of Gitty's bakery truck.

I'll kiss you again if you bring a half dozen, she texted.

Not that she really planned to trade her virtue for muffins, but Gitty's baked goods were amazing. She and Gitty had been friends since childhood and Gitty's muffins had only gotten better with time.

"Come on back," she said to Ryan. "We'll wait by the pool."

As soon as she sat down, however, he disappeared back into the shadows. Not that there were many shadows as it was morning, but the man had mad skills. While she waited for Declan, she got on the internet. Last night's event had drawn lots of coverage, with multiple celebrity gossip sites running pieces on the "clinch" between her and Declan. There were photos, too—photos in which she almost didn't recognize herself, so his celebrity makeover lessons must have stuck more than she'd thought.

In one shot they were laughing and the lighting somehow made them seem as if they stood in a golden spotlight. The beads of her dress had caught on his arm and the expression on her face—

She looked dazed. Swept off her feet. Drunk on the man holding her in his arms. Was there a twelve-step program for people with addictions to handsome charmers?

"I should have pushed him overboard when I had the chance," she said to herself. Ryan wisely remained silent.

Her email inbox overflowed with messages from people she hadn't talked to in years, asking if it was true that she was dating the movie star Declan Masterson. Some wanted introductions, while others pitched scripts. Her fifth-grade teacher had acting aspirations.

A buzz of sound rose up from the front of the house. People shouting and calling things, among them Declan's name. She tried not to listen to the questions too hard because they were all variants on last night's horribly embarrassing interrogation. A few long minutes later, her father's housekeeper showed Declan out to the pool. He held a cardboard tray of coffees in one hand and a bakery box in the other.

He passed her a coffee, then offered her the box. She tore it open because, as last night's pictures proved, she'd already misplaced her dignity. Gitty's muffins were the ambrosia of breakfast baked goods and Declan had been true to his word. He'd brought her six muffins—and a caramel brownie.

"I'm considering accepting his apology," she told the muffins. "Even if you brought your evil twin, Mr.

Brownie, with you." She picked a muffin out and bit in. Oh, God. Had she moaned out loud?

Declan laughed. She totally had.

"Why a brownie?" she asked around a mouthful of muffin.

"Muffins are just cake masquerading as a health food." He smiled wickedly. "So why not just eat cake?"

She looked in the box. "But you brought me muffins and a brownie."

He held up a paper bag she hadn't spotted, probably because he'd kept it hidden. "I'm saving the cake to bribe you with."

He handed a coffee to Ryan and then sat down opposite her, hands wrapped around his own cup.

"So," he said.

Her stomach dropped. Was the press coverage that bad that he felt the need to ease into it?

Or did he just feel guilty because he'd been the one to dip her into that clinch and he was the movie star? "How bad is it really, on a scale of one to catastrophic?"

"It depends on how you look at it. And I do mean you. Not me, not Ryan, not your dad or anyone else. The story is great for the race. It gets eyes on our race cause, people are donating and it's reading as romantic."

"The story being how your famous self swept a local girl off her feet in a whirlwind Hollywood romance?"

He winced. "Yeah. That part. Honestly, they'd like it even better if one of us was royalty and had a castle."

"Can't help you there," she said. "We're short on castles in New England."

He eyed her cautiously. "It will mean attention. The reporters will run what they can and dig into your life. It's not as if you've done anything newsworthy or embarrassing, so the digging won't get them far. At the end of the day, we're just two people who shared a dance and maybe a little more. They'll run the pictures from last night on a loop while they try to get something more interesting. As long as we both keep our clothes on and don't do anything stupid—"

"Like climb a balcony naked," Ryan interjected.

"—it will be fine," he finished.

She had a feeling that her having dated a soon-to-be-indicted embezzler probably wasn't going to fly under the radar. Should she break the district attorney's demand for secrecy and tell Declan? Not yet, she decided. Not until after she'd made a phone call and asked if she could.

"Actors and actresses date outside the industry," Ryan offered. "It's actually not uncommon at all. People like who they like and as long as you two don't do anything new to draw attention, things will calm down."

She studied him. "How do people live with that kind of scrutiny? And I mean, how do they really live with it? Can you even go out and buy toilet paper like a normal person?"

Declan shrugged. "It's one of the price tags on getting the chance to do a job I love and that matters to a whole lot of people. Plus, it doesn't always happen overnight like this. You sort of get eased into it and don't realize it's happening until you make a midnight run to the convenience store and get snapped in your pajamas. Ryan's the best and he knows how to shut things down when interest in my girlfriend gets out of hand."

"Fake girlfriend," she said. "And how much does Ryan cost?"

"That doesn't sound like a no." He nodded to Ryan

and the bodyguard strolled away. Apparently like all men they spoke a secret language. "And I've got the cost covered. Don't worry about it, okay?"

"I'm new in this fishbowl. Be gentle."

He grinned. "I can do that."

She was *not* going to think about that. "But is it always this bad?"

"Not usually," he admitted. "But there's an upside." He held out his phone so she could see it. The race organizers had set up a set of cutesy thermometers, one for each boat. As donations came in, the thermometers filled. Declan and Charlotte's thermometer was completely full now, when she knew for a fact that it had only been half-full yesterday afternoon. Last night's kiss-and-flirt strategy had borne fruit.

"Tell me what you want to do," Declan said. "I know it's a lot to ask, living with paparazzi. If you want to pull the plug, we can."

"You'd quit the race?"

His eyes held hers. "If that's what you want, yes. I'll quit. It's your call. I can put out a statement. We can find you a new partner."

"Why did you agree to participate?"

"J.J. asked me to do it," he said. "It mattered a whole lot to him and making him happy had some upsides for me."

Right. She sucked in a breath. "I don't want you to disappoint him."

"Just tell me what you want," he said again.

That would be a very long list. "I can't pretend I'm going to like having all those people watching us, thinking they get to weigh in on what we're doing. But I'm thinking it's time I stopped explaining so much. Even if I like playing by the rules and having a plan, I think there could be a time to not do those things."

"Fortunately," he said, "I'm an expert in operating without a plan."

"Right."

He shrugged. "So maybe you should just go with your gut. Fly by the seat of your pants. Live life planless."

"And be your fake girlfriend and race partner?"

"Yeah." He was smiling at her again, and damn but he was hard to resist. "And my first official act as your fake boyfriend is to invite you on a picnic. Date me, Charlotte."

Charlotte's life was neat and predictable, with no room for tall, handsome movie stars who got mobbed by paparazzi and who kissed indiscriminately at public events. *Get used to it; you can't take back kisses and it's just a lunch with a guy who's practically a business partner!*

"Food," he coaxed. "Even better than muffins."

That was an outright lie, although she'd bet that the movie star version of lunch did not involve her beloved—and budget-friendly/spill-proof—PB&J. She looked back at her not-boyfriend and wondered how well she could pretend that she was comfortable with his luxury lifestyle. *It's not weird; it's just lunch and you can get through it. Free food!*

"Lunch with my hot fake boyfriend? Of course, we'll have to actually leave the house and I'm apparently under house arrest."

"All I'm hearing is *hot* and *arrest*," he said lazily.

She rolled her eyes at him. "Don't tell me. Your favorite fantasy costume is the naughty cop."

He mimed zipping his lips, which was a problem because the man's mouth was dangerous, open or shut. She'd learned last night what he could do with those lips of his when he wanted.

"Come on." He got up and held out his hand. "Brave the horde out front with me and I'll feed you. Put something in your stomach besides sugar and caffeine."

"Those are the most important food groups." She had a horrifying revelation. "You're not one of those California healthy living advocates are you? Because that's grounds for an immediate breakup."

The bastard actually laughed.

"I do whatever the part requires."

She waved a hand. "But does it ever require doughnuts? What's the point of being a star if you can't eat what you want?"

He laughed more, so of course she followed him, and leaving her own house was even more of a production than she'd imagined. The photographers had multiplied like bunnies, but without the cute factor. These were jostling, shouting, downright rude rabbits.

Declan's mouth brushed her ear. "Say nothing."

No problem. Given that she had goose bumps from just that little touch, she was fine with taking a perpetual vow of silence. Declan guided her past the paparazzi, directing a polite smile and a "no comment" at the yellers. Better yet, Ryan somehow turned himself into a human wall, deftly inserting himself between the cameras and the two of them. In less time than she'd thought possible, Declan was handing her into his sports car. She took a deep breath and yanked the door closed.

"Good to go?" he asked her, sliding into the driver's seat.

"Yes," she said. "I'm also fine with fleeing, running away and driving like a maniac."

She decided not to think about getting back into the house. Somehow, it was hard to worry when she was riding shotgun with Declan, probably because the crazy wild chemistry between the two of them was a greedy thing that left no room for other feelings.

Declan seemed to know where he was headed, so she just enjoyed the ride and the scenery, both inside the car and out. He radiated strength and she amused herself by making a little mental list of all the things to admire about him: A pair of powerful forearms bared by the shirt he'd rolled up above his elbows. His thighs in those damn blue jeans. And—she might have leaned forward *just* a little—the pair of black, beat-up work boots he wore. He'd flashed her a smile at that one, but it was worth it because her list also included his sense of humor, his willingness to listen and his insistence on looking out for the people who came into his life, even if they were temporary additions.

After he'd made a quick pit stop to pick up a picnic basket, a covert exchange behind one of the Vineyard's fanciest hotels that had her looking over her shoulder for spies or hit men, he took her to a private beach. She knew it was private because a half dozen signs and a security guard said so. Feeling a bit like a trespasser, she slid him a glance as they were waved in.

He grinned. "Called in a favor."

"Right," she said lightly. "Because you're best friends with the rock star owner?"

"Producer owner. We've worked together."

Great. He knew movie producers and rock stars. She loved her life. She did. But moments like this just reinforced that in his world he was a on a first-name basis with famous movers and shakers, while she might peep at them for five seconds in the local coffee shop.

The private beach was a creamy stretch of sand squeezed between the ocean and sand dunes. Other than four white Adirondack chairs lined up to take in the view, there was nothing but sand, the tide washing in and some impressive bluffs at the far end.

She immediately kicked off her sandals and pointed to his feet. "Take them off."

"Woman, you keep trying to get me naked."

She laughed. "You're wearing far too much clothing for the beach."

"You know you could just ask me to undress? For you, the answer would be yes." He toed his boots off and tossed them onto a chair, holding his hand out for her own sandals which he set more carefully next to his.

"So what's the beach plan?" And then when she gave him a sideways glance, he shook his head. "You know you have one. We'll work you up to going fully planless in baby steps."

"Walk first," she said. "Then we eat all the food."

"Got it," he said and tugged her down the beach.

After a few minutes, she repossessed her hand. She assumed it was automatic on his part, but her glamorous new haircut was in no way windproof and she had hair in her mouth and her eyes—possibly up her nose, too. She twisted her hair up, securing it with a hair tie she'd had the forethought to stash on her wrist.

And not an elegant twist or a fancy chignon. Nope, she wound it like spaghetti on a fork and let the ends flap free. It was at-home, sweats-and-a-T-shirt hair, but Declan just tucked an errant end under the tie and smiled. "Pretty."

The casual gesture made her feel shockingly good.

They wandered down the beach, poking at interesting piles of driftwood and letting the chilly surf foam around their ankles. She picked through the shells mounded at the hide tide line, slipping a particularly pretty scallop and a pearly moon shell into her pocket. Heat tingled through her when he threaded his fingers through hers as they made the return walk back up the beach.

A black SUV that she assumed belonged to Ryan was parked next to Declan's sports car, but the bodyguard himself was out of sight—probably not far though.

She and Declan spread out a plaid blanket on the sand and he grabbed the picnic basket.

"Let's start with dessert. Just in case we get interrupted."

He shot her a lazy grin. "By paparazzi?"

"Sure." She tugged at the basket he was holding. He had promised to feed her, after all. "Or an alien space invasion, the apocalypse, whatever. Give."

This earned her a laugh, but he set the basket down and flipped open the lid. Then he pulled out a huge, chocolate-filled plastic clamshell. "A backward meal? I like it. But be warned—I know the secret to winning your heart now."

"You started it," she said. "When you brought cake for breakfast."

Okay, so Declan had actually only handed over the six muffins and their brownie best friend, but he'd claimed to have cake.

It turned out that *cake* actually meant *cupcake*, but she could work with that, especially when he handed her a plastic fork. He'd planned well for a man who claimed to hate planning.

Ignoring the teasing glint in his eyes, she dug in. And moaned. He laughed. "What? I have sunshine, the ocean and delicious cake. What more could a girl want?"

He rolled over onto his stomach and rested his chin on his arms, watching her. "I have an idea."

She pointed the fork at him. "Nope. No sex talk."

"Who, me?"

Yeah, him. He was such a problem. She wished that the breeze that kept the summer air from getting too hot would do something for her libido. She ate her cupcake and tried to figure out a solution to her Declan Masterson-sized problem.

The source of all that heat rummaged in the picnic basket, pulling out his finds: Cold lobster rolls with thick chunks of pink-and-white lobster in white rolls. Plump strawberries. And Boston cream pie cupcakes, because her movie star not-boyfriend definitely knew his way to a woman's heart. She tried to find something to be irritated about but, really, he'd gotten everything exactly right. After he'd made her a plate and then served himself, they lounged on the blanket and he told her stories about the film industry.

"How did you get into acting? No. Wait." She made

a face. "That has to be a question you've answered hundreds of times."

"I've never told you."

"Was it something you always wanted to do?"

"I liked the stunts," he said. "Never met a dare I wouldn't take. I was that kid who jumped off roofs and rode his bike down the crazy hill while standing on his head."

"Did you really do that?"

"Jumped off the roof at my elementary school, jumped out of my bedroom window twice, jumped out of the belfry at church…"

She stared at him. "How are you not dead?"

"Excellent reflexes. Sheer luck," he said promptly. "Although the belfry thing did not go well. I thought I could rappel down the outside hanging on to a bell rope, but it turns out the bells were all on some kind of automated system and a computer rang them. I'm sure you're shocked to hear that everyone thought I was a natural fit for the whole stuntman thing. Which was convenient, since J.J., my father, owned a production company. He was very popular on career day at school because he specialized in blowing things up."

Turned out, Declan was good company. He asked questions about her own work and then told more stories about stunts gone wrong and ridiculous director demands. He also had plenty to say about actors who thought—wrongly—that they could do their own stunts without any training. He was far more self-deprecating and aware than she'd given him credit for. She found herself blushing more than once because he'd been places and met people, accomplishing things that most people only dreamed about.

"Why are we even here having a picnic?"

"I'm feeding you." He passed her the last cupcake, proving he was at least a gentleman.

"But *why*?"

Laughter danced in his eyes. "Maybe I like taking care of you. Maybe we were both hungry and you'd eventually need to eat something and yet there you were, trapped by paparazzi and it was all my fault. Are you always this suspicious?"

"I'm never suspicious and that's a problem."

"So you trust me completely?"

"No. I don't trust you at all, but I'm terrible at remembering to question what people tell me. I don't fact-check. Why would I go around assuming everyone is lying to me until proven otherwise?"

She threw up her hands. Unfortunately she was still holding a cupcake, so instead of making a point, all she accomplished was painting a streak of frosting down her cheek.

"See? I'm a mess. All the makeover lessons in the world are not going to turn me into a glamorous Hollywood swan."

"Charlotte," he groaned, swiping his big, warm fingers over the frosting tattoo she'd given herself. "You're wearing your cupcake."

His thumb swept over the corner of her mouth.

She froze. Was he—

"You're a perfect mess," he said and it didn't sound like a complaint. At all.

Then he pulled her into his big, warm body and kissed her.

Ten

There was kissing and then there was *kissing*, the kind that made a woman forget where she was and all the reasons that kissing a man back might be a bad idea. Sensation zigzagged through her body, warming her belly and other parts of her. He coaxed greedy sounds from her mouth as her hands tangled in his hair, Charlotte holding him close because this was amazing and she wanted more. She tasted frosting and the sea, sunlight and something warm and male that was all Declan. She didn't hold back either, which was part of that trusting-too-much-and-too-fast problem that she had, but how could she resist? Everywhere they touched, there was heat—and they were touching *everywhere*. It was crazy how much he wanted her, and that was before she pushed him back onto the blanket and he rolled her on top of him.

Flashing her a happy grin, he wiped the rest of the frosting off her cheek with his thumb. She laughed—and kissed him again.

Her heart raced because if he was this good at kissing, what else was he good at? And how could anything feel better? Kissing Declan was like a scene from one of his movies, and yet she knew this was really, really happening. Her knee pressed against sun-warmed sand where she'd slipped off their blanket, but her other knee was tucked against his hip. With all of him stretched out beneath her, she could feel his interest—and he had a whole lot of interest going on.

"I want you." He said it straight out, tipping her chin up so he could see her eyes. He didn't hesitate.

"I want you, too." Truth. Her voice caught in her throat as he adjusted their fit together, bringing her flush against him. She could move away, she knew. He wasn't holding her any tighter than she wanted—and that was another problem.

"Are you sure?" he asked and she came back to reality faster than she would have liked. The kissing was so perfect, as was the holding and the way he fit her against him.

"You mean right *here*?" The sand was warm and they were allegedly alone, except possibly for the invisible Ryan, but sex with a movie star on a beach might be too adventurous for her. *Sex with Declan*, her libido teased. *You know you want to.* Her brain, however, refused to turn off any longer. *You're on a beach! Sand! Paparazzi! Public witnesses!*

"Just kissing today," he said. His thumb rubbed the corner of his own mouth and came away with icing he must have kissed off of her. The heated look in his hazel eyes said he didn't mind. He licked his thumb.

"That sounds like a good plan." She tried to straighten up, to shift herself off him to a safer distance.

His warm hands tugged her back down, sliding up her back and beneath the cashmere cardigan. Calloused fingers skimmed up the line of her spine and then back down again, tracing patterns on her lower back.

"You feel so amazing here." He drew a small circle and she shivered. "And here."

His fingers moved upward, exploring the curve of her waist with lazy intensity. When he drew his fingers slowly upward, he rolled their bodies again so that he came down over her, bracing an arm beside her head. The pressure of his body on hers made her arch upward, had her making space for him between her legs because that felt even better than his kisses. She wrapped her legs around his hips as he bent toward her again, his mouth tasting the sensitive skin of her throat. With him holding her right back, she got lost in his kiss.

When he pulled back with a rough sound of pleasure, she stared up at him. "Wow."

"Yeah," he said. "Definitely wow. Too wow. We're not doing anything you aren't ready to do."

"Believe me," she said, "I like doing this with you. Consider me one-hundred-percent on board with this kissing plan." But what if it wasn't as good for him as it was for her? She should ask, shouldn't she? "But what do you want to do?"

"Everything, Charlotte. I want to do everything with you."

Everything sounded amazing.

Everything sounded perfect.

She breathed out and tried to marshal her thoughts. Her eyes got a little starstruck looking at him. Kissing Declan was crazy. A magical kind of crazy. No one had ever made her feel this way, and pretending to love him would be far too easy.

"But we don't have to do this fast," he said.

That was the worst plan she'd ever heard… Every inch of her—and quite a few inches of him—were voting *hard*, *fast* and *right now*.

"We can take our time," he added. "And Charlotte, I'm going to need a *lot* of time to appreciate you right."

She laughed. "I'm not that complicated—plus you're clearly on the right track."

He sat up, gently depositing her on the blanket beside him. "I'd like to get this right, even if right now I feel like eating you up and racing right through all the talking and getting to know you stages. Going to bed with you will be amazing."

Will be—not *would be*.

She could tell from the way his eyes darkened that he was thinking about it—imagining the two of them in a bed, starting with kissing and ending with all the delicious, dirty things the two of them could imagine. But he was right that some things shouldn't be rushed. Plus, they'd both rushed into their last relationships and she couldn't bear to repeat that mistake.

"You're good at this," she said.

"You certainly make me want to be." He brushed a light kiss over her mouth. "Come on. Let's get you back to town."

"Race prep," she agreed. "We need to win this thing next week."

He tugged her carefully to her feet. "You bet."

Somehow, though, she felt as if she'd lost.

Eleven

Charlotte sat in the *Cupcake* and tried not to think about the ways today could go wrong. The little boat that Declan had christened after last week's kiss flew across the water, the start line well behind them. *Think positively.* They had a ten-minute head start thanks to their fundraising efforts, so they'd not only started at the favored end of the line upwind but they'd avoided getting stuck in a pack of boats. They had a written game plan for how to sail the racecourse and she'd memorized the sailing instructions provided by the yacht club—and stashed her race binder in the aft storage locker just in case she needed a refresher. Her one job was to monitor the VHF radio on the race channel. Both she and Declan were wearing non-inflatable racing PFDs over their sailing kits so even if she did fall overboard, she'd float. And the man himself had one hand on the tiller and the other doing… Well, she didn't know what he was doing because she still hadn't mastered the finer points of sailing.

She tightened her death grip on the boat as it surged forward and the race start line swung back into view as Declan tacked them into the wind and *Cupcake* shot ahead. The rapid change of direction made her stomach lurch. But knowing that nineteen other boats and sets of racers waited behind them for the starting horn, she welcomed every drop of speed Declan could coax from their boat—especially since they had nine hours of sailing in front of them. The race course would take them around Martha's Vineyard and the first boat to cross the finish line won. Winner takes all—there was no prize for second. Thanks to the dark clouds piling up on the horizon there almost hadn't been a race today. The ocean was equally unsettled, waves slapping harder and harder at *Cupcake*'s sides.

Her brain unhelpfully flashed her back to that other summer day, the one where the ocean had done its best to kill her. She'd been splashing around in the shallow water when another kid had dared her to race out to a mooring buoy and back. Once she'd got to the buoy, tapping the white ball enthusiastically, she'd discovered she was alone. A quick squint back toward shore had revealed a mostly empty patch of beach as everyone had been lured elsewhere, likely by the promise of s'mores and hot dogs because they'd been on a picnic and those things were fun.

By the time she'd shoved off the buoy and headed back toward shore, she'd been tired—and caught off guard when she'd ended up in a riptide. And possibly she'd panicked and tried to compensate by kicking harder for the beach. Maybe she would have remembered in time that you had to swim diagonally to get out of a rip current, that there was no brute-forcing your way through it, but she hadn't.

So no, she didn't love being out on the ocean. She loved the Vineyard, loved the dunes and the rugged shoreline. Dry land was awesome and it was home, even if a rather terrifying amount of ocean surrounded it.

Declan watched her calmly. "Are you doing okay?"

The man saw too much. His job here was to be the pretty face and muscle, a job at which he excelled. He wore dark cargo shorts in some kind of quick-dry material that hugged his thighs, a sailing jacket with the race logo and a high-tech T-shirt that stretched deliciously taut over his powerful chest and shoulders. Sunglasses hid his eyes, but she knew amusement sparkled in them. Amusement—and something else. She hadn't decided yet if that *something else* was affection or caring or just good, old-fashioned lust.

"Just fine," she lied.

His lips twitched. "I can go faster."

"Wasn't that the plan?"

"Didn't know if it was in the binder." A smile teased his mouth.

"Planning is important," she said. For instance, in addition to the PFD cinched around her waist, she'd dressed in multiple race-crew-approved quick-dry layers because her internet research and their practice sessions had taught her that sailing was wet and not infrequently cold. She probably looked like a sausage, but at least she was a room-temperature sausage.

"Sure is." He adjusted something, and dear God, they were, indeed, moving faster. "Ride's going to be less smooth, though."

"The goal here is to win. You do know that, right?"

"I do," he agreed. "Just thought you might like to work up to it."

It being the mind-numbingly, terrifying speed that the *Cupcake* achieved under his command. When she finally opened her eyes, Charlotte couldn't quite drag a full breath into her petrified lungs. Wind tore at her mouth and nose.

Okay, so she still had some oxygen, but how Declan could laugh as if this was his idea of a good time, she had no idea. Two hours later, she remained clueless. She'd spent the time shifting from one side of the boat to the other at his calm orders. Once she caught sight of sails behind them, but for the most part they were alone on the ocean. Declan was, she grudgingly admitted to herself, good at this. She was coming to think they'd win and then they'd—

She didn't know what came next, other than somehow weathering the storm that would break when George's felonious behavior emerged. People would blame her, rightly. She'd been all in favor of hiring him and then she'd dated him. Agreed to marry him. Trusted him too fast and too much. Hopefully the prize money would alleviate the worst of the hurt for her kids.

She used the next hour to sketch out a mental plan. She'd deposit the check, there would be revelations and then, well, she wasn't *quite* ready to watch Declan sail out of her life. The man might be irritating and arrogant, but he was also dependable and rock steady. Not everything was a race with him and part of her was disappointed that they hadn't gotten as far as bed yet. Okay. So she knew exactly which parts those were— some very good, very fun parts of her anatomy—but her head and her heart liked how he wanted to take them slow and not rush things.

By the time they'd dodged the ferries that kept Martha's Vineyard connected to the nearby islands, the wind was pushing them along and the channel currents ran fast enough in the sound to have Declan keeping a very watchful eye out. Maybe, she thought as she shifted yet again at Declan's low command, she might just take a chance—a small, manageable, not too publicly risky chance—and ask him to do something with her after the race. Not a date. Like… Okay, so exactly like a date. A chance to explore a normal relationship with a man she liked and found attractive. Could you have a normal relationship with a movie star? What would they do if they weren't bickering or engaged in a little bit of semi-friendly competition?

The clouds piling up on the horizon now were green tinged and the air had a heavy, expectant feel, not least because fog had started settling between them and the shore, hiding her view of dry land. She'd memorized the map as if knowing the landmarks and the depth soundings would help when she no longer knew where she was. The ocean needed street signs.

"Are we still ahead of everyone?" she asked. They'd only had a ten-minute lead and Declan wasn't omnipotent, no matter what his online fan club believed.

"Not what I'm currently worried about," he said.

"Maybe you could tell me this story has a happy ending."

He gave her a look. "We're going to be just fine."

At the sound of the calm assurance in her voice, she shook her head. "Are you lying to me? Because I've heard that tone before and it always means that I should expect something to go epically wrong."

"No shit," he said.

"Are we okay?"

His voice gentled. "Okay, so the ending will be fine. I promise. The middle may get wet and rough."

She waited for full-on panic to strike, but something about Declan had her pressing pause on her anxiety. And she might not have been big on trust—or trusting her own abilities to get herself out of a sticky situation—but he just calmly did the next thing. And then the next. She managed to take the yellow rain slicker he passed her without visibly freaking out.

"Find the local weather broadcast." He nodded toward the VHF radio. She wished it was a magic teleporter and not basically a walkie-talkie connecting them to the yacht club and the Coast Guard, but, well, she'd make do. She fiddled with the radio, found the right channel and listened in disbelief. The sort of storm they were predicting sounded both sudden and apocalyptic. She switched back to the race channel, checking for new transmissions from the race committee. Sure enough, they were warning the competitors to tune in to the weather channel.

"Don't they call these things off if the weather is bad?"

He nodded. "Sure, but I've sailed through worse."

She narrowed her eyes. "That doesn't help." And then, because it was like inching past an accident on the highway where she'd try not to look but her eyes would go there anyhow, she had to know. "Like what?"

"Hurricane-force winds. Frostbite race on the Chesapeake Bay that turned out colder than four layers of fleece could handle. Wall of water hit the boat once and we heeled over until I was kissing the sea."

"You know what?" she said. "Forget I asked."

"Right," he said. "But you're overlooking one key point."

"What would that be?"

"I was on each of those boats and now I'm right here."

"So you're a bad luck charm!" She threw up her hands. "I should throw you overboard like they did that guy in the Bible."

"*Good* luck," he corrected. "Or, more accurately, lots of practice and experience. I've done this before and I've got this. I've got you. Okay?"

"I'm not really okay about any of this," she said honestly.

"Trust me?"

She'd certainly tried not to. Her trust track record was a series of crashes, wipeouts and epic fails, so his ask was a big one, one she'd been fighting for a while now. She met his gaze and he smiled, the corners of his mouth tipping up as if there was something even remotely happy about their current situation. And yet... Of course he would take care of her when no one else had her back. Because that's who he was.

She tightened her grasp on the edge of the boat just in case. "Okay."

When the thunderstorm started she was still saying *okay*, but the word was a substitute for the F-freaking-bombs she wanted to drop and had a much higher pitch than normal. No amount of bad weather sailing videos on YouTube had prepared her for the reality of a small keelboat in the middle of a thunderstorm and she was starting to have serious doubts. The *Cupcake* rose and fell, her prow slapping hard against the water and sending spray everywhere. The whitecaps had whitecaps, for crying out loud, and the increasingly stronger gusts of wind made her feel like they were headed nowhere fast.

"Charlotte?"

"Yeah?"

She tried to find a silver lining. Maybe that the lightning hadn't struck them? She counted that as a win. It made the hail that was bouncing down seem downright benevolent. And hey, the hail was merely pea-sized and not the golf ball–sized monstrosities that dented up the Vineyard's cars and roofs indiscriminately. This was totally manageable, even if it felt like she was being attacked by a swarm of icy killer bees.

"You know I won't let anything bad happen to you, right? I'm still right here with you." He gave her a small smile, which was totally inappropriate, in her opinion. If ever there was a moment to panic, now was the time.

"Are you God?" She stabbed a finger in the direction of the purple-and-green clouds—which were no longer on the horizon but somehow overhead and simultaneously all around them.

"You'll be okay," he repeated.

She groaned. "I'd feel better if we were having this conversation on dry land."

"Yeah," he said. "Me, too."

Well. Crap.

A new gust of wind jarred the *Cupcake*. The radio squawked feebly. The race officials had apparently misjudged the rapidity with which the storm would hit. They'd expected the racers to be around the island, heading into the final stretch before bad weather struck, but that seemed less and less likely.

"Since I'm still working on my trust issues," she asked, "how anxious should I be right now? On a scale of one to ten?"

He adjusted the sails some more. "I've run worse races."

"But those were bigger boats, right? With an entire crew of people who actually knew what they were doing?"

"You know what you're doing," he said. "You've got one job right now."

"Right," she shuddered, grateful for her water-resistant layers. "This is where you tell me it's to trust you. That's not working for me, although it's a cute line."

"The worst race ever, we had lightning strikes landing all around us and each time I touched the tiller, I got a shock."

"Did you let go?"

He gave her a level look. "I held on when I had to."

The thunderstorm/apocalyptic avalanche of rain wasn't letting up, though. Even she could tell that. After another eternity of minutes, he turned them toward the island. "We can make a run for shore or we can try to speed up and outrun the weather. I'm voting for shore."

"Did they call the race off?"

"Not yet."

"But—"

"It's just a race," he said. "And while they'll likely call it soon, I'd feel better if we played it safer now."

She couldn't help but notice that *safer* didn't seem to mean *slower*. Or *calmer*, *less nauseating*, or any one of a dozen other words she would have preferred to use to describe their situation. Instead, he sent them flying faster and faster over the water, driving the *Cupcake* toward the island.

The boat dove sharply and she lurched sideways, off-balance. Her feet slid on the water-slick deck and her view shifted abruptly from Declan's concerned face to the water, and suddenly she was staring at the waves. Which were far too close.

Declan cursed, barking out an order to hold on. *Too late*, she thought, *but a really good idea.*

The boat pitched again and then she was sliding fast, fast, fast toward the edge and going over. At first all she could see was water. She'd sworn to make no more choices she would live to regret, but that promise didn't cover this situation. God, she was going to drown for real this time. If she'd known that dying was the plan, she'd have gone for it with Declan, spent less time working and more time doing other things.

Living, for instance…

She went under, the wave closing over her head, and she panicked, unsure which way was up. The PFD wasn't enough. It felt like she'd been jammed inside an enormous washing machine and God had pushed the button for the Rinse cycle. Her heart pounded and her lungs shrieked in warning as her oxygen supplies dwindled faster than she'd have thought possible, making her regret all the time she'd spent on board talking rather than breathing.

She was going to drown.

There was no other option.

A powerful arm hooked around her waist and pulled her inexorably upward, or at least in the same direction as the body attached to the arm. She let it happen.

"Charlotte!"

She choked on the water in her throat. Salt water stung her eyes. God, she needed to breathe. To get out of the freaking water. "Where is the boat?" she wheezed out, sucking in air.

Declan pulled her to him as another wave closed over them.

"Breathe in and hold," he ordered. "Close your eyes."

She did exactly that, clutching his arm as the relentless water crashed over and over them. *Don't breathe in. Don't drown.*

He pulled them both back up to the surface, angling her until her back pressed against his chest and he was between them and the next wave.

"This is what we're going to do." He turned them and then he locked an arm around her chest, towing her with him as he swam in long, powerful strokes.

"Swim for the boat?" she asked hopefully. She looked, but she couldn't see the boat. For all she knew it was just on the other side of the waves battering them.

"We're going to swim for shore. The boat's flipped by now and righting it will be exhausting with just the two of us."

"Fantastic. And shouldn't we stay with it? In fact, why didn't you stay with it?" She tried to look over Declan's shoulder, but he was too big. And there was just water, water and more water because apparently she'd fallen overboard into the nightmare version of the *Ancient Mariner*.

He grunted and surged forward in the water. "You went overboard."

"And? We didn't both have to drown."

He groaned. "Are you trying to convince me to ditch

you in the middle of the ocean, Charlotte? Because it's not going to work. I promised you I'd stick with you. Yeah?"

She expected him to point out that it was her fault they were alone in the middle of a very pissed off ocean, but he didn't, possibly because they were—okay, so mostly *he* was—swimming for their lives. Recriminations would come later. She started kicking her feet. "Okay."

"Great. Charlotte?" And then when she nodded, and might have whimpered just a little, he said, "Your job here is to hang on to me. You don't let go. I don't let go."

"That's it?"

He swam for a long moment. "Here's the plan. No more talking. Save your breath for when I've got you ashore and then let me have it. Yell. Cry. Whatever it is you want to say, I'll listen."

"So shut up and swim?"

"That's the plan."

It was one thing to fall off the boat, an involuntary action, one that she couldn't stop once started. It was another thing entirely to keep swimming. The waves never stopped battering them and she lost count of the number of times water closed over her head. *Don't stop swimming. Kick your feet. Declan's not worried.*

Not that she really knew what he was thinking.

She felt better assuming and he talked to her, despite the *no more talking* part of their plan. He told her that they were getting close, that she had this, that he could see the shore and a Four Seasons hotel. She might have called him out as a liar on that last one, but instead she swam and she tried to do her part, blocking out the regrets that beat at her. Imminent death had a way of making a girl think about what she hadn't got around to doing. She wished she'd taken a chance on Declan. Taken a shot at *them*.

When her arms and legs flagged, he growled in her ear, "Don't quit on me, Charlotte."

"Not—" she sucked in sea water, coughed it out "—princess? No cute but annoying pet name?"

"You keep trying until we get to shore, I'll call you whatever you want."

True to his word, he didn't let go.

Twelve

Declan had never believed that life emulated the movies or that the intensely physical stunts he'd mastered for that work had practical applications. Today, though, he drew on all that training and then some, pushing his body through the waves, pulling Charlotte with him. It was the hardest thing he'd ever done and not because of the twenty-minute swim in grueling conditions. Keeping Charlotte safe was more important than anything. He'd promised her, and he wouldn't be the next person to break a promise made to her.

Charlotte was clearly terrified. She hated deep water, hated being forced to depend on him to get her to shore. He got that. She made him feel vulnerable, too. Because for once it wasn't enough to be the strongest or the fastest, the most disciplined or fearless. He could shoot a gun, drive at near-suicidal speeds, fall from almost any height and work an explosion. What he didn't know how to handle was Charlotte.

She wasn't fearless, but she fought. She let him take the lead, but then she played an amazing best supporting actress.

When his knees hit solid ground, he told himself he felt nothing but relief. He'd hoped for some elation and, even better, for the next step in this not-plan to reveal itself to him. Instead, the sickening fear that he'd failed Charlotte almost kept him there on his knees. There were so many things he should have handled differently, from not calling the race sooner to relying on the race committee for historical weather analysis. The sudden storm had blindsided him. And then she'd gone overboard and he'd abandoned the standard protocol of trying to bring the boat around to pull her out and just gone straight after her.

He staggered upright, setting her down beside him but keeping an arm wrapped around her. The cold pebbled her exposed skin.

"Just a few more steps," he lied.

She gave him a look. "And then there's a heated SUV waiting to whisk us off to a luxury hotel for a spa day?"

Okay, so she understood more than he wished she did. Rather than answer, he tugged her toward the beach, moving swiftly through the surf that swirled around their knees. The rain had finally started to ease up, but now they were out of the water, cold would be a big factor.

"You got any idea where we are?"

"Lost. Shipwrecked. Auditioning for a really bad TV reality show?"

She was trying to put a good face on things. He ad-

mired that about her, although he wished like hell that
she'd been wrong on the first two counts. The narrow
strip of beach hadn't come with a convenient street sign.
He'd also have taken a parking lot, or any sign of civi-
lization at all. Instead he got wet sand bordered on one
side by the still angry ocean and a marshy inlet on the
other. He saw reeds and grass bending in the wind, a
bedraggled lot of seabirds hauling ass overhead and
more rain. What he didn't see were lights, human habi-
tation or a solution. His current best option was a rather
stunted tree fifty feet up the beach.

He drew her up the sand toward the tree because
something was always better than nothing. His years
in the foster care system had drummed that lesson into
him. They had the clothes on their backs. They hadn't
been blown off course to Canada or Cuba. And—he
patted the dry bag clipped to his cargo shorts—he still
had his wallet and his cell phone in its waterproof phone
case. Unfortunately, when he pulled it out, he didn't
have service.

"Hey," he said, gently tugging her underneath the
tree. It had gray bark that made him think of elephants
or seals and the branches offered some protection from
the rain. She sank onto the sand and he bent down to
look her in the face. "Stay here a moment for me, okay?"

"You want to define *a moment*?"

At some point they needed to talk about why she
thought people either wouldn't choose to stick around—
her ex-fiancé came to mind—or wouldn't come back
for her, but now wasn't that time.

"I promise I'll come back, but you're cold and tired
and I can do this quicker on my own, which is better
for both of us. You've fallen off a boat, swum for your

life, and that SUV didn't get the memo or it would be here, so let me take care of this, okay? Let me take care of you, Charlotte."

"You did all those things, too," she said, but she sat down on the sand where he indicated, wrapping her arms around her knees. She'd lost her sailing shoes and crew cap during their swim, but the rest of her was still covered in layers of quick-dry fabric. "I'm okay. Are you okay?"

"Yeah." He pressed his mouth against her cheek, not liking the way she shivered or the paleness of her skin. She was tapped out. "Hang on for me."

"Go." She waved a hand. "Find us a rescue party."

He considered her for a moment, then draped his own, larger sailing jacket around her. "As you wish."

After the longest ten minutes in the history of time, Declan jogged back. Charlotte was happy to see him, as her already low tough girl reserves were frozen through and through. She hadn't even started to process what losing the race would mean.

"You still okay?" he asked. She didn't know what he expected would have changed, but she warmed at the concern in his voice. Given her current state as a sea salt–flavored human popsicle, she'd take that warmth.

"Okay enough," she said grimly. "And—thank you." She grimaced. "For coming after me. For sticking with me."

"Jesus, Charlotte." He stared at her. "You need to work on your expectations."

Sure. She'd do that later—after she'd warmed up all the way and could forget just how close she'd come to dying. *Again.* Since she preferred not to think about near death, she made a give-it-up gesture.

He sighed. "You want the good news or the bad news?"

For the record, she *never* wanted bad news.

She looked around them but, nope, no Four Seasons had miraculously sprouted while he'd been gone. She also didn't see a car or any other sign of a rescue party. "The bad news is that we're still lost and shipwrecked. Oh, and we're out a million bucks, so perhaps we should start hunting for buried treasure."

A smile lit up his face. "Yeah, but that's also familiar news. The good news is that I found us something better than a tree."

"Hey," she said, patting the tree trunk. "Don't malign him. He's doing the best he can."

"You want a lift?" He patted his back. "Hop on."

She shoved to her feet, shaking her head. Of course she wouldn't let him carry her. He'd already dragged her butt to shore, so she needed to pull some weight here. "I've got this. Where are we going?"

He gave her an assessing look, then nodded slowly. "Not far."

He tucked her into his side, putting himself between her and the wind that blew off the ocean and straight through her wet clothes. A hundred yards up the beach, he cut away from the shore and through the dunes to where a weathered set of wooden steps cut through the sand. The thunderstorm was moving off, but so was the daylight.

The weathered house perched at the top of the steps. *Shack* might have been a more accurate description as it looked as beat up by the elements as she felt, with shingles peeling off the roof and a wide, wraparound porch full of ancient rattan deck chairs that listed suspiciously eastward and downward. She spotted no lights and, more disappointingly, no cars. They were still on their own.

Declan tugged her up the steps and straight to the front door, where he proceeded to bang hard enough to make the frame shiver and shake. She wasn't surprised when no one answered. The Vineyard was dotted with summer places, owners coming and going as life and their work schedules permitted.

"You might want to turn your back," he suggested. "If you're squeamish about felony B and E."

Beggars, choosers and all that. Shrugging, she swiped a large decorative conch from its place of honor and handed it to him. "Here you go."

He raised an eyebrow but took the conch shell, which had either come from the granddaddy of all sea snails or been manufactured in China, and broke them in with a quick, hard blow to the doorknob.

Gathering the remnants of her energy, she followed him inside gratefully. The first floor was all one room, with windows looking out at the ocean on one end and a massive stone fireplace on the other. A large, L-shaped sofa and several mismatched armchairs were grouped in front of the fireplace. It was homey and unpretentious, furnished with finds from flea markets and attics. She wasn't quite sure what the protocol was when you'd been shipwrecked and stranded on an absent homeowner's beach.

Declan held up a palm and moved swiftly up the stairs to the second floor. Normally she would have protested his easy assurance that she'd follow his lead and stay when told to stay, but she wasn't sure her legs would carry her up the stairs. She could hear him calling out a greeting, just in case the homeowner had somehow slept through their felonious entry. Sleeping sounded like a good plan. The best ever plan, in fact. She staggered toward the sofa, debating planting on it, wet clothes and all. There were no light switches and the air held a damp chill, even though it was summer. It was just their luck to have found a cabin with no heat or electricity.

Declan returned with an armful of blankets before she could summon the energy to lie down. "Strip."

"Don't I get dinner first?"

He grinned and tossed her a packet of dried fruit and a handful of granola bars. "Ask and ye shall receive. Strip. I'll build a fire."

Getting out of her wet clothes suddenly seemed like the best idea ever, so she peeled off her sailing leggings and the sodden scuba hoodie while he gave her his back to give her some privacy and built a roaring fire faster than she would have thought possible. When he turned back around, looking pleased as warmth started to wash over the room, she could barely hold in her sigh of pleasure.

Just admiring the scenery, she told herself. Who knew that what she really got turned on by was a guy who knew how to scavenge for groceries and build a fire? Looking wouldn't hurt her.

And then when he busted her, she pretended it was the fire that had caught her interest. "Impressive, Hollywood."

"Lots of practice," he said. "My brother and I lit a lot of stuff on fire when we were teenagers."

Casually, he stepped behind the sofa and stripped off his own clothes. She would have liked to see more, but the sofa back was high and he had to work to get the wet cargo shorts and T-shirt off. She caught a flash of some kind of thinner undergarment before she remembered she wasn't looking.

"If you came over here and lent a hand, you'd get a better look," he said. "I'm not the shy one."

"Cute," she said, tempted. But getting them both warm, dry and fed was more important right now. Plus, her blanket toga wasn't exactly sexy lingerie. She padded into the kitchen that was tucked away in the back, trying to ignore the wet *squelch* as he took it all off, and rummaged around for two mugs and some water from an ancient plastic five-gallon jug.

When she came back, he'd wrapped a blanket around his hips and legs and had a second draped over his shoulders. It should have made him look ridiculous. Instead he looked ridiculously hot. Her libido promptly decided that they should hold a naked, sexy celebration of life.

Tamping down that thought, she shoved one mug at him. "Here."

He took it and patted the sofa cushion beside him. "I saved you a spot."

Instead of teasing her further, though, he handed her a granola bar and pulled his phone out of his dry bag, holding it up for her to see. No signal. They were good and stuck. Ignoring his invitation, she paced back and forth, ate her granola bar and failed to come up with a plan.

Imagine that.

Right now all she had was a list of disasters: a lost

race, a wrecked boat and no way to fix the hole that George had put in Martha's Kids' budget. How could she not freak out?

"Hey." Warm fingers braceleted her wrist, slowing her. "Come and sit with me, Charlotte."

She let him pull her down onto the sofa and up against his side. She liked sitting with him. Being next to him. Okay, so she just liked him. A lot. And since thinking about that just freaked her out, she returned to her first topic. "No one knows where we are. We lost the boat. We lost the race. We just committed felony B and E. As days go, this one sucks."

"It could be worse," he said.

"How... No. Wait." She slapped a hand over his mouth. "Don't tell me how it could be worse. That's need-to-know information only."

He pressed a kiss against her palm and gently shifted her hand away from his mouth. "Let's make a list, Charlotte. Next steps. What we'll do tomorrow."

She stared at him. And lied her ass off. "You may be used to catastrophes and disasters, but this is my first time."

"I'll be gentle," he said solemnly. "What's the first thing we need to do after we fall off the boat and into the ocean?"

"Get to shore." She gave him a look. "Find help. Take the world's longest nap."

"We've done the first one," he said. "And now we're helping ourselves. We've found shelter. We've got a fire. And hey, I've even made us dinner."

"Sure," she said, "but since no one knows we're here, we're also stranded."

"But we've got six things crossed off." He mimed striking through a line.

"Thank you again," she blurted out. Was it smooth? No. But it was one-hundred-percent heartfelt.

"I was happy to help."

"I—" She had no idea how to explain. And did she really want to?

"Don't like water. Yeah. Believe me." He scrubbed a hand over his still damp hair. "I get that. I know you don't like to talk about things, but maybe you should talk about this one?"

It was possible that he was right.

She stared up at him, assessing her chances of getting out of this with her dignity—and her heart—intact. Not only was she far too close to his spectacular chest but, just possibly, she'd used up all of her luck on the whole falling-overboard-and-not-drowning thing. "Okay. So first of all, I suck at thank-yous, but I owe you this one. Thank you for jumping in after me." She paused. "It was a stupid thing to do and you could have still won the race."

"You wanted me to sail on and leave you there?" He sounded incredulous.

"Well, I was more thinking you could have fished me out before you sailed on. One-handed? Like a knight leaning down from his horse?"

He looked down, angling his face until he could see hers. "I told you I wouldn't leave you. I made you a promise."

"Well. Thank you. Again." She paused. "Wow, this is awkward."

"Do you know many people who would leave someone alone in the water? I'm asking for a friend here."

Was *she* his friend?

"It happens," she said carefully. "And as I'm an adult, I'm trying hard not to judge those people, okay?"

"Not okay," he said. "Not ever. Also, Charlotte?"

"Yeah?"

"It will never happen on my watch and never to you."

As promises went, it was a doozy.

"I knew you liked me, Movie Star."

"Charlotte." The way he said her name, rough and intense, melted something cold inside her. "Did something like this happen before?"

Thirteen

Charlotte opened her mouth. Closed it.

Declan knew that look. He'd seen it on his own face before he'd learned to hide it. It was the look of someone who'd been left. He hated that for her.

"I got left a lot as a kid," he said quietly. "My biological dad left first, before I was born, so my mom always had work to go to—errands, a second or a third job. She'd leave Nash and me alone in the apartment with food in the fridge and a list of things we weren't to do or touch. It took longer and longer for her to come back, though, so eventually I'd break the rules. In hindsight, she likely tried the best she could, but I was a kid and being alone was scary. I thought it was something I'd done wrong."

"Was that when you went into foster care?"

"Yeah. And then a couple of years later, she died in a car accident. J.J. adopted me eighteen months after that."

"That had to have been hard," she said softly.

He didn't like talking about those days. He'd been vulnerable then and now he wasn't. Except that for Charlotte he might make a tiny exception. "I learned a lot in the years between my first home and J.J.'s. Mostly how to be tough and to stand up for myself. I got into a lot of fights and figured out that I liked the adrenaline rush. I liked it even more when I realized that fighting could be strategic, that it had a rhythm, a choreography of sorts. It all prepared me for the stunt work that led to my career, so I'm not complaining."

"I'm glad it had a silver lining for you, but I'm sorry, too." Her mouth quirked up ruefully. "And I know that isn't the right thing to say, but yeah, that's me. Queen of the conflicting emotions and poor phrasing."

He pulled her closer. "J.J. was… Well, J.J. was his own kind of challenge. He chose to bring me home and then he spent a lot of time after that laying out the ways in which I'd turned out to be a poor choice. And when he got mad or criticized, I'd throw myself into my next adventure since I'd already disappointed him. I'm guessing your childhood wasn't picture-perfect."

She wiggled back an inch and stared at him. "Wait. Was your sharing a clever trick to make me share? Because I'm going to need more details if we're trading life stories."

He let out a low laugh. "Busted. But Charlotte, please tell me?"

"I was at a beach party," she said quietly. "The adults were up on the bluff. It was a pretty important event. There were some people my father wanted to do business with and he'd warned me about staying out of the way. So I went down to the beach with the other kids and we horsed around in the surf. Nothing too out of control—it was all perfectly safe."

He had some thoughts about the safety of unsupervised kids on a beach, but he kept them to himself.

"One of the other girls dared me to race her out to the mooring buoy and back," she continued. "I agreed. I was always a bit shy and this girl was super cool. So there she was talking to me and actually asking me to do something with her. No way I'd refuse plus I was an awesome swimmer and I was totally going to kick her butt. We got in the water and someone called the start of our race and I really went for it. I didn't realize until I tapped the buoy that I was out there alone."

"She turned back?"

She shook her head. "She never swam at all. She was laughing on the beach with her friends. I never found out if the dare was a joke or if someone she was actually friends with had distracted her and she forgot about me. They went back up on the bluff and then I had to swim back alone. There was a rip current and I was too tired and inexperienced to get myself out of it. Eventually one of the other parents did a head count and figured out I was missing. When they spotted me out in the water, they called the local rescue team who retrieved me. My father was pissed off that I'd caused such a commotion."

"That was a rough day," he said. "There's no excuse—"

"But there's a silver lining to my story," she said.

He stared at her. "What?"

She frowned. "Well, I learned that I hate the ocean, suck at racing and don't care for front-page coverage in the local newspaper. Which pretty much makes us opposites."

They were opposites if she meant that he loved the ocean, won every race he entered and had millions of social media impressions. None of that was the important stuff, however. Today had gone wrong in more ways than she knew. In losing today's race, Declan had lost J.J.'s test. No more CEO, no more Masterson Entertainment. He set that thought aside for later, pulling Charlotte closer. The storm that had wrecked them had moved off, the rain slowing. He could head out, find help. And yet—

She twisted in his arms and looked at him. "Thank you for coming after me."

"We discussed this," he said roughly. "No thanks necessary."

He would have said something more but her new position had her straddling his thighs. And then she rose up on her knees, his legs between hers, and things lit up faster than the sky during the storm.

"Declan?" She leaned down, bracing her hands on his shoulders.

"Yeah?" he asked, intending to suggest a getting-rescued plan. Instead his arms went around her back, sliding beneath her blanket and across bare skin. The heat of her set him on fire, filled him with a new purpose and sense of connection.

"I want this chance."

And then she leaned down, set her mouth on his and kissed the hell out of him.

A chance to do something new.
To do something. To go for what she wanted...

She kissed Declan because they'd almost died and because time was precious. She wasn't going to waste it, not when the man she wanted was here, they were both naked and they were trapped together. If that wasn't a sign from the universe, she didn't know what was. So she kissed him, sinking into the heat and the desire, the rightness and sense of belonging she tried to share with him, with her mouth and her hands cupping his face so that she could have her way with him. A groan tore from him when her tongue found his and she might have made a few answering sounds of her own.

She was breathless, as was he, when he pulled back, locking his gaze on hers. "When you want to stop, say stop," he said. "I won't take advantage of you."

While she appreciated him putting the control in her hands, she needed to make one thing clear. "You're not taking advantage. And the key word here is *if.* If I want to stop, I'll say it."

He nodded, his hands tightening on her back. "That's another promise, Charlotte."

The man and his promises were killing her.

"So you want to kiss me," he continued.

Warmth pooled in her belly. Declan was always in motion, always doing something. Now he was waiting.

For her to make up her mind.

To choose him.

He reached up and tucked her hair behind her ear. "Is that all you want to do?"

"It's the first thing on my list," she said. "But it's a long list and there may be crying if you don't have a condom."

"Yes," he said roughly. "In my wallet and thank God for dry bags."

"So prepared." She laughed and trailed her fingers over his face, the roughness of the stubble that covered the hard line of his jaw making her shiver. He was strength and heat in a delicious package and—

He drew her mouth back to his. Bracing her arms on either side of his head, she sank into his hold. A hand cupped the back of her head, strong fingers threading through her hair. And then he kissed her, a kiss that started out gentle, his teeth nipping softly at her lower lip, and then deepened as his tongue swept inside her mouth.

She'd never felt this kind of desire. She wasn't a casual kisser, hadn't dated much and didn't jump into a relationship feetfirst—or heart first. But this man made her burn and ache for something more, as if he was the happy ending she'd dreamed about. True intimacy took trust and she didn't trust easily. In fact, she didn't trust at all, and that had her holding back rather than letting go.

George had been a mistake. He'd charmed and flirted his way into her life, and then when he'd told her he wanted more, that he wanted *forever*, she hadn't seriously considered whether or not she could give him that—if she even *wanted* to give him that. And while she'd been hurt and humiliated when he'd left her, she'd also, on some level, expected it.

People didn't stay. People *left*.

But, her heart protested, *Declan is different. He came after you.*

And the truth was, he had. Every single time it counted, he'd come after her.

"Still a yes," she said against his mouth. "And also please, thank you and hurry up."

"Yeah," he said roughly. "Me, too."

That one word said it all, didn't it? He slid a big,

strong hand through her hair, pulling her back so he could kiss her some more. *Yes* to this moment. *Yes* to this night. *Yes* to the two of them and exploring whatever that could mean.

At some point during all of the kissing, when their hands had both wandered south, he turned them both, tucking her beneath him on the couch. She tilted her face back up to his, letting him see exactly how much he made her feel. "You make me crazy."

"Good," he growled. "Because the feeling is mutual and it's also crazy new. This isn't a one-night thing for me and I don't want to watch you walk away from me in the morning—but I also don't know what you're feeling or what you want."

She laughed against his mouth. "We want the same things."

She knew that because he was hard against her and no way was he close enough. She slipped her hands around his back, tugging him nearer. "Make love with me?"

He groaned against her mouth. "This wasn't exactly how I imagined our first time together."

Laughter and heat bubbled through her body. "Did you actually make a plan for it?"

"I've had a few fantasies, Charlotte. I want you, but I imagined showing you how special you are by doing this somewhere better."

"I'm safe, we've got a fire, we're both here," she said. "That sounds perfect to me."

"Yeah?"

And then his mouth was gliding over hers again, kissing her softer and then deeper as he teased her lower lip, her cheek, then the curve of her throat as he loved his way down her body.

The blanket fell away and Declan smiled, a wicked, sexy grin at the sight of her bare body. "Beautiful." His hands stroked over her body, learning what made her sigh, what made her giggle, the touches that made her whimper and whisper his name before making some noisy demands of her own.

"Beautiful here, too." He touched her lower, his fingers trailing slowly over the soft skin of her thighs and then between them with a care and skill that had her whole world focusing on him, breathy sounds escaping her mouth. He made her want and want and want.

"Declan," she murmured, wrapping her legs around his, rocking into his touch. She was close and she needed him inside her. "I'm—"

"Beautiful," he whispered, his mouth chasing the teasing touch of his fingers. He found her bare breast, kissing and sucking as his fingers slid into her and she forgot to hold back and just held on to him. And when he moved lower still, his mouth replacing his fingers, she got completely lost in the erotic tension, her soft, breathy sounds mingling with his rougher, hoarser murmurs.

"Are we still good?" he asked when he'd explored every inch of her with his hands and she'd said, "Yes, more," and "Oh, God," and "Now?" more times than she'd ever expected. And then she'd come apart for him, fireworks exploding behind her eyes.

Her body quivered, wanting all of him, ready to do it again.

"Can you be better?" The man did like a challenge, after all.

He grinned at her. "Better. Or very, very bad depending on what's on that list of yours."

And then he pressed her down, using his mouth and his fingers to show her all the ways a woman like her could enjoy a man like him. A long, long time later when she'd come for him a second time and was floating in a sea of pleasure, warm and boneless, she heard the sound of a condom packet being opened and then he moved back up her body and came into her, proving that she was no more done with him than he was with her.

Fourteen

Later, as they lay there, tangled up together, Charlotte wondered how she was supposed to put herself back together. The rain was stopping, the steady drumming on the roof easing up, and she could hear the ocean again, the waves pounding on the shore. There were a million things they should do, but mostly she never wanted to move again. Who knew sex could be so amazing?

Declan's quiet "Be right back" sounded promising. She watched through half-closed eyes as he got up and dealt with the condom and the fire before returning to scoop her up on top of him. She curled into him gratefully because part of her was still cold.

"Why weren't we doing that sooner?" she asked.

He gave a rough laugh and pulled her closer still, until his chin rested on her head and his hands were locked on the small of her back. "If we'd done this any sooner, we wouldn't have been out there on the water. I'd have spirited you away to my castle tower and locked us in."

"That sounds rather grim. I'm not sure castle towers figure prominently on my fantasy list."

"My private tropical island then," he said. "And feel free to tell me more about this fantasy list of yours."

There was a note in his voice she couldn't quite make out. "Do you actually have one of those?"

"A castle? No." He traced her cheek with a calloused hand. "But I'll get one if that's what you want."

"Just you will do," she said.

That's a big ask. She shoved away the unwelcome thought. She had tonight, didn't she? And she'd promised herself that she wouldn't waste chances, not anymore.

"You can have all of me, Charlotte."

"Really? All of you?" she asked. Certain parts of him were making it clear that all of him was ready to repeat what they'd just done.

"You bet," he said and then he kissed her and one thing lead to some very pleasurable other things so that the fire was dying down again before they'd finished.

Charlotte drifted off eventually, or possibly she fell asleep, because one moment she was wrapped up in the very sexy Declan as he pressed kisses against her hair, which had to be a Medusa-worthy tangle of salty waves, and the next the room had that not-quite-dark light it got when the sun was almost ready to start making its morning appearance. And Declan was still holding her.

The fire had gone out altogether, but she was plenty hot, possibly because she was being held against Declan and there was a whole lot of bare, warm skin to enjoy.

One arm kept her close, while the other was tucked beneath his head. She admired the downright gorgeous line of his deliciously scruffy, morning-after jaw before she realized that he was awake and watching her right back.

Oh, God.

They'd slept together. She turned that thought over in her head: the boating disaster, the terrifying swim to shore, his insistence that nothing would hurt her while he was there and then the far more personal turn things between them had taken. The kissing. The naked touching. The sex. The amazing, mind-blowing, best-ever sex.

That was going to be a problem.

And also? He was still watching her.

"Hey," he said finally.

She stared at him some more.

"You look like you have something to say."

She was sure she did. She was equally sure that it would take days—weeks—for her to form a coherent thought. "What?"

"Are you okay?" he asked.

"I don't know what to do here," she admitted. "And honestly, this doesn't seem like your usual scene."

"Holding a beautiful woman? Or holding you specifically?"

Her breath caught. "That might be too much honesty."

"Because holding you is really working for me," he said.

Her heart nearly stopped. She was starting to realize that he saw her as more than an island fling and she couldn't bear the thought that she'd get her hopes up and then he'd leave and it would all turn out to be a misunderstanding or a mistake.

Charlotte looked nervous. This was not a look Declan was okay with, especially when he was holding her and they'd just had the most amazing sex of his life. *More than that*, he thought. His brain tried out a brand-new pair of words: *making love*. When he'd first been matched up with her for the race, he'd been irritated. And attracted. And yeah, he realized, eager to score points with J.J. with his makeover dare.

Charlotte still didn't know about that deal with J.J.

When he'd dared her to do the makeover, she'd believed he was an arrogant Hollywood know-it-all who'd decided to torment her for his own reasons. And sure, he'd had reasons. Plus, her irritation had amused him, making him mad on her behalf that the people in her world routinely overlooked her because she wasn't splashy or putting herself out there. He'd unintentionally misled her about his reasons for racing, and truth was, as he'd gotten to know her, he'd lost sight of how J.J. would see it: that Declan had found himself the perfect cure for his rakish, playboy reputation.

The flushed woman in his arms, warm and completely undone and open, wasn't Instagram ready or perfect in any of the ways Hollywood prized, but her eyes, full of affection—and possibly something more—met his and he knew he was on the verge of something amazing if he just reached for it. They fit together and he loved it. She felt like she might just possibly be the most important adventure of his life, and yet he hadn't been as open with her as she had been with him. If she'd been just a casual hookup, the J.J. deception wouldn't have mattered.

But it wasn't casual. Not on his part, not any more.

He tried to imagine how that conversation would go. *I've mentioned J.J.? And how he's a bit of a controlling bastard? Funny story, but he offered me a once-in-a-lifetime deal. If I pass his test, he'll hand over the family company to me. I have to prove I'm reformed, respectable material by winning a high-stakes philanthropic race in Martha's Vineyard.*

And oh yeah, we lost that race. Badly.

They'd have to have the conversation, he knew, but not here. Or now. If it went badly, she couldn't leave, at least not safely, and he'd never do anything to make her feel unsafe or threatened.

This was too important, even if he wasn't sure yet what *this* was.

He moved his hands over her, soothing, tucking her in closer, making sure she was as happy as he could make her. And also to distract her, because he was certain she was already thinking and planning.

Sure enough, she looked at him and grimaced.

"At least you didn't get caught scaling a balcony naked this time."

"If I'd known it would be like this, I'd have been outside your room every night."

"I live on the ground floor." She laughed, clearly thinking she'd deflected his interest in having a serious conversation. And truth was, he didn't want to talk about what had happened. He didn't do emotions and he certainly was no expert in opening up. But even he knew that what they'd just shared was more than amazing sex, and he wanted it to happen again.

He wanted it to happen with her.

"This is nothing like that," he said.

"Good," she said. There was an awkward pause.

While she hopefully thought about what he'd said, he leaned up on one arm so he could check out her face. Mostly, he wanted to make sure that she was still okay, at least physically. Falling off a boat could be really bad. She could have hit her head or an arm, injured herself and not noticed it. He'd seen stuntmen take a blow and keep right on working for hours and hours until the adrenaline wore off and their bodies gave out. He never wanted to see Charlotte get hurt.

Leaning over her, he brushed his hands over her face, then down her body, relieved to find nothing wrong. "You sure you're okay?"

This time her amused laughter was genuine. "Yes, doctor. Or was that a comment on your bedroom skills?"

"Hey. If I didn't get it right, we can keep practicing." Nudging her chin up with his thumb, he kissed her.

Fifteen

It wasn't the sun pouring through the windows that woke Charlotte up. It was the banging on the front door. The banging—and the voices. She and Declan had fallen back asleep in a cocoon of firelit darkness and the warmth of their bodies, a sweetly private space that had terrified and amazed her.

She liked Declan. That thought was the first that swam up to the surface. Possibly more than *liked*, a little voice whispered. *You got naked with him; you had sex and you opened up in* all *the ways. That's the* other *L word.* Her heart decided this was a good moment to start banging around inside her chest, as if it had something to contribute to the conversation. Or maybe that was whoever was outside the house. The house they'd *broken into.* She shoved that thought aside for later. Apparently orgasms did wonders for her anxiety because she couldn't remember the last time she'd felt so relaxed. Kissing. Touching. Out-of-this-world sex. Those were good things, but she loved non-sex time with Declan just as much. After all, they'd only had sex for a handful of the hours she'd spent with him. Sex would have been simpler.

Easier to maintain her distance.

Which was non-existent at the moment.

She was wrapped up in his arms, one of his legs thrown over hers. This position was vying for her favorite Declan position (although he'd certainly shown her a few new favorites last night) as her face was pressed against his chest. His heart beat beneath her cheek, solid and steady. And just in case she hadn't paid enough attention to his chest last night, she brushed a few bonus kisses over the smooth, sun-bronzed skin. She might have licked him. Just once. Okay, twice.

The real problem was that she wanted to do it all again. And then again and again. He held her as if she were precious and he was completely bare. The blanket slipped off one hard, muscled shoulder and of course she couldn't help looking at him. He was something so unfamiliar, someone she liked—*loved,* her traitorous heart whispered. *This isn't a simple case of the likes.* And maybe, just maybe, he had the same kind of curiosity about her and they could see where this went. She was turning that thought over in her head when the banging sound started up again.

That was bad.

Or good? Had they been found already? Declan cursed, tightening his arms around her and shifting her off and onto the couch. He tugged a blanket around her even as he got up.

"We've got company," he said, cursing some more. "The rescue party's here."

While she hadn't expected to wake up to the first day of forever with Declan, she also hadn't imagined that they'd be rousted by a large search party. Somehow, when she'd imagined a rescue, she'd imagined a much smaller—and less curious—number of people.

Declan tugged on his cargo shorts and strode over to the door. Despite their drenching in the ocean and rough swim to shore, he looked amazing. She drank in the muscled perfection of his chest, the strong line of his back as he turned, and the tousled mane of hair. And oh, God, if he was wearing just a pair of shorts, she was naked.

He yanked the door open, blocking the doorway with his body. She had a bad feeling that it was too little, too late. After a brief consultation with whoever was out there, he shifted his attention to her.

"We've been rescued. Brace yourself." Then he turned back around to what sounded like a hundred people and said, "Charlotte needs a moment."

He shut the door and crossed the floor toward her, a small smile tugging at the corners of his mouth.

"This is totally your fault," she said. "I'm not the one who got me naked."

He gathered her clothes from where he'd laid them out to dry and she pulled her leggings and T-shirt on under the cover of the blanket, blessing the quick-dry fabric for living up to it marketing promises. The noise level outside grew. While she donned what armor she could, Declan swiped his T-shirt from the chairback where he'd left it.

"Am I decent?"

"Yeah." He gave her a quick check. "Charlotte—"

"Because," she interrupted, "I've learned enough about social media to know that I do not want to go out there with my butt hanging out."

He put a finger on her lips. "I'll take care of this."

"Hey," she said. "We're partners."

"Not a dictatorship," he agreed. "Partners. And as the expert partner on scandals, I'm warning you that things are going to get a little rough out there, but I'm not going anywhere. Got it?"

"O-okay." It took her two tries to get the word out.

He nodded and then gently pulled her outside and onto the porch. Jeez. She tried to smooth her hair back, to pretend that nothing had happened when everything had changed. People in various uniforms milled around the house and there were even more members of the press. She tipped her head back and, yep—that was a helicopter circling overhead. People greeted Declan by name, offering coffee and jackets, EMTs and assistance. Ryan popped up, moving fast, and the two of them were halfway to him when she spotted the *Cupcake* washed up on the beach below them.

Oh. My. God.

Their poor *Cupcake* was in pieces. She lay on her side in the surf, the mast snapped off and the sails dragging in the water. Panic squeezed her chest, the truth hitting her. The race was lost and she wasn't going to win the money that Martha's Kids needed to stay afloat itself. All she would be able to do was say "I'm sorry" a billion times.

Declan squeezed her fingers. "I'll be right back."

She scanned the crowd while he walked away to exchange a few low, terse words with Ryan. There was no one she really knew, although she could put a few names to some faces as it wasn't a huge island. The search and rescue team went down to the beach to salvage the boat or whatever it was that people did with shipwrecks. Was there AAA for the boating world? She was still trying to figure it out when Declan handed her a cup of coffee, slipped a pair of shoes he'd magicked up onto her bare feet and shepherded her toward the helicopter that had landed some distance away on an open, grassy expanse.

The press, which had been pushed back down the driveway, started yelling out questions again, asking what had happened.

He barely paused, keeping her tucked into his side. "Bad luck and the storm. You can't win them all."

"How do you feel about losing the race when you were was so far out ahead?"

"What do you want to say about the rumors circulating that you're dead? And that the Academy is planning a tribute?"

"Charlotte! Can you describe Declan's heroism for us? Did he save your life last night? What was it like being stranded with Declan overnight?"

Everyone turned to stare at her. Why hadn't someone invented an invisibility cloak? Cameras clicked as she scrambled into the helicopter. She'd never ridden in one before, but desperate times called for desperate measures.

"For God's sake," Declan muttered. "Next they're going to ask if we've sold the movie rights."

"Can we just go home already?" she asked.

"On it," he said. "I'll take you anywhere you want to go."

Charlotte's usual life called for minivans or beat-up SUVs, so the helicopter was perhaps one new thing too many. Declan's playful exchange with the reporters replayed in her head. Last night he'd said he saw them together, but he'd given no hint of that to the reporters. Since her options were limited, however, she let Declan settle a pair of headphones on her. Moments later the private pilot had them airborne, Martha's Vineyard falling away from them. *Lifestyles of the rich and famous*, she thought hysterically.

After a brief flight, the pilot swung them back over the ocean and toward Edgartown. All too soon they were settling down on the concrete helipad behind the house. A late-model BMW was parked next to Declan's sports car, along with at least a dozen other cars. The pilot killed the engine, and after the blades had stopped spinning, Declan came around to help her out.

"Hi," he said, wrapping his hands around her waist and swinging her out. She grabbed his shoulders, suddenly off-balance. "We really need to talk."

She slid her hands off his shoulders. "Right now?"

All she wanted was more coffee, a hot shower and a bed, because she was pretty sure she didn't want to deal with messing up Martha's Kids' second chance yesterday. Plus, she looked about as bad as anyone would after nearly drowning, going without hot water for twenty-four hours and spending the better part of the night making love instead of sleeping.

"There's a lot of interest in what happened yesterday. TV coverage, social media, that sort of thing. People want to talk to us, hear what happened. We've sort of come back from the dead. At least that's how the headlines read."

"Everyone thought we were *dead*?"

He nodded. "And now we've been resurrected."

He wrapped an arm around her shoulders and started toward the house. There was a crowd of people pressed up against some kind of barricade at the end of his driveway. A roar went up when they spotted Declan.

A mound of flowers, stuffed animals and glass candles had been piled up against the barricade. She'd known that Declan was a star, but she hadn't realized until now what that really meant. Lots and lots of other people thought they lo—*liked*—him, too.

"Is that what you wanted to talk about?"

"Not really." He steered her toward the door and then stopped, bracing an arm by her head and leaning in. She rested her forehead on his chest, numb with exhaustion. "But there are lots of people in there. J.J.'s doing media."

"What? Why?"

Declan's mouth brushed hers. "Because he's a Hollywood mogul and this is great exposure. Because he's an ass. And probably also because he is my father and he thought I was dead."

"So he's giving interviews?"

"Some people like to talk."

Great. She was going to meet J.J. wearing yesterday's salt-soaked sailing kit. She was just grateful that she couldn't see what her hair looked like. And yet somehow Declan managed to look rugged and handsome, like a victorious Viking seafarer home from conquest.

Paparazzi called their names, asking Declan how they were.

Declan didn't slow. "Right now, I need to get the woman I love inside, warm and dry. That's my only priority."

She froze. *Love?*

He tugged her inside while the reporters yelled and cameras went off. Inside turned out to be equally chaotic. Doors were thrown wide, people with headsets rushing in and out and rattling off brief, incomprehensible details to each other. The living room had been turned into a temporary television studio.

A tall, broad-shouldered man in his late fifties strode toward them. His dark hair was streaked with silver, the waves ruthlessly tamed. He wore an open-necked white dress shirt tucked into tailored suit pants and a Rolex glinted on his wrist. He had the same aura of command as Declan, but with a harder, more predatory edge.

"Introduce us," he said to Declan.

Declan just looked at him. "Charlotte, meet my father, J.J. Masterson."

"Mr. Masterson."

"Call me J.J., Charlotte." J.J.'s hand engulfed hers in a firm, quick grip. "You're even lovelier than your pictures. Tell me my son took good care of you last night."

Not sure what to say, she stuck to the truth. "He did."

J.J. nodded. "He knows the right thing to do on the water."

Declan stared back at his father and they engaged in a silent conversation, exchanging tense looks.

"Not well enough," J.J. said with a nod, as if he'd just

had the last word in that silent conversation. He winked at her. "But we'll fix that. There's an entire team to take care of you. You're a prize and Declan here knows that."

Charlotte felt the breath catch in her throat. "Pretty sure I cost him the prize."

J.J. looked at her. "Not yet, darling. Not yet."

What?

Then he turned to Declan. "Good job, son."

"Not now," Declan growled. "We're not getting into this right now."

J.J. waved a hand and walked away with someone who wanted to run a media schedule by him. Charlotte thought she recognized an online reporter from a popular morning show, along with a woman she'd seen on prime time at night. She was too tired to sort it out.

"What you said out there," she said. "Right before we came in?"

"That the only thing I need to do right now is take care of the woman I love?"

"Yeah, that," she said faintly.

Declan just watched her.

"You love me?"

"Yes." He brushed a kiss over her forehead.

She inhaled, legs quivery with exhaustion. "You love me."

"You don't have to say anything right now." He winced. "Or at all. But whenever you do want to say something, I want to listen. Right now, though, I want to get you somewhere you can lie down and be quiet. If that plan's okay with you."

"I love you, too," she whispered.

Sixteen

"You think a free meal is worth all this effort?"

Charlotte jumped, pressing her palms against the windows lining the hotel ballroom. The glass was pleasantly cool despite the decidedly midsummer temperature outside. The sun had barely gone down, but it was dark enough to see the man reflected in the window behind her. *Declan.* Her tuxedo-wearing, smiling Prince Charming. Her heart did some much less startled, sexier jumping.

"Definitely not." She tilted her head back, resting it against his shoulder. "But we're pretending that we're not sore losers, right?"

"Speak for yourself." He caged her in his arms, pressing a kiss against the top of her head.

The man in the reflection was extraordinarily handsome in his designer tuxedo, the black jacket stretched across powerful shoulders. He belonged in this room of politicians and celebrities, wealthy Vineyard residents and donors, who had come together to celebrate the winners of the charity race. Surprisingly to her, the woman standing with him looked as if she fit, too.

Charlotte fit.

Almost, impossibly so, or at least with this one, wonderful man. His stylist had pulled a dark rose tuxedo jacket for her with a low-necked white bodysuit that scooped her breasts up and then up some more. The matching floor-length pencil skirt hugged her curves and set off a pair of Christian Louboutin sandals in a glossy red that echoed the cherry-colored lips the makeup artist had given her and the Edwardian rubies surrounded by clusters of old mine-cut diamonds that dangled from her ears. She looked good, she decided. Better than good. Despite everything, she looked— happy.

Or at least, happy enough.

She was trying to decide if Declan regretted their loss when he smiled down at her. Okay. So definitely probably almost certainly teasing. After their disastrous end to the race three days ago, Charlotte suspected that almost everyone would have excused them from tonight's awards banquet. Most of the other racers had been forced to abandon the race, although none in quite such a spectacular fashion. In the end, the winner had been the last boat to start and had managed to wait until the worst of the sudden storm had blown through before leisurely sailing to the finish line entirely alone. It was the classic Tortoise and the Hare story. No one had expected a member of the local Coast Guard and an international dressage competitor to win. Declan had come in for more than his share of good-natured teasing.

And far too many people had spent the evening staring at her and Declan, speculating about what had happened in that beach house. She told herself that words were, well, just words. She'd ignore them and get on with her life. She'd almost managed to stay off the internet this morning and avoid reading the latest article on how Declan had bravely plunged overboard after her and brought her nearly lifeless body to shore.

Awkward.

But she'd congratulated the winners and tried to pretend that she was merely politely disappointed to have not landed the grand prize for Martha's Kids. The orchestra hired for the night launched into a waltz.

"One last chance to play Cinderella," she said.

He pulled her a little closer, giving his head a little shake. "You'll always be my queen."

She laughed. "Cheesy, much? Also I'm almost certain that you accused me of being a princess. Have I been promoted?"

He groaned. "You're not going to let me live that down, are you?"

"No." She grinned up at him.

"I was wrong." He nipped her ear gently, smiling. "You're far more than just a princess."

"Ruler of the universe, that's me." She smiled back at him.

For a hopeful moment, she thought he'd be content to flirt or dance. Instead, he exhaled roughly and his smile turned rueful. "Charlotte?"

"Are you going to ask me questions I don't want to answer?"

"Probably."

But he didn't ask, not right away. Instead he held her, letting her hide behind his broad chest from the billion people crowding the ballroom—all of whom were staring at them or talking about *how heroic Declan was* and *what do you think* really *happened that night*? She wondered what they would think and say if they knew about George's sticky fingers. After a minute, she took a breath and stepped out of his hold to stand next to him.

He slanted a careful glance at her. "Answer me this. Are you okay?"

"Can you be more specific?"

"Charlotte," he growled.

"You already said that," she whispered. His presence beside her felt so good, forming a sort of human shield even though she knew that she could stand up for herself. But no matter how safe and protected and, oh man, so wonderful—white knight Declan was, this side-by-side thing was even better.

"I'm waiting," he murmured. He took her hand casually, running his thumb over her knuckles.

"We lost." She shrugged as if it were no big deal, as if she weren't...overwhelmed by losing that one last chance. Overwhelmed with guilt and remorse, regrets and what-ifs.

"Spectacularly," he agreed.

"So there's no million-dollar donation for Martha's Kids. We could have used that money."

He nodded once. "For your summer camps. So Maggie can be a kid and Jay can eat himself full for once."

She loved that he'd really listened to her, and she warned herself not to get any rash ideas about confessing. She needed to keep the truth to herself so she didn't make things worse, because the district attorney hadn't given her the green light to talk about the case and because maybe, if they found George fast enough, there would be some money left. It was about trying—and failing—to protect her summer kids, keeping them safe from the mistakes the adults in their lives made.

But this was *Declan*. Keeping secrets from him felt wrong. She weighed silence against sharing, and knew that she couldn't keep this from him, not if they were going to have any kind of a real relationship. She had to trust him with everything, including the not-so-pretty parts of her life.

"We have a budget problem," she admitted. "I mean, there's never enough money when you're a nonprofit, right? That prize money would have been... Well. Let's just say this Cinderella is going to have a lot of work to do when she gets home from the ball. Because—"

She stared at him, willing the words to come out of her mouth. To tell him the entire truth. *Because my ex-fiancé stole everything. Because I trusted when I should have been asking questions. I'm so, so sorry. And—*

And she had no idea what to do next.

"Charlotte?" He ran his fingers along her jaw. "It's okay. Whatever it is, it's okay."

It so wasn't, but apparently she was going to chicken out. "Let's not talk about it, okay? Not tonight. It was just a race and a crazy idea of mine." *Like the crazy idea of us.* But he'd said he loved her.

He squeezed her hand gently. "Isn't that what Prince Charming is for? Fixing all of his ladylove's problems?"

"News flash. You're not a prince, Hollywood." She brushed a kiss over his mouth. "Can we leave?"

"Sure." He let out a low laugh. "I think we've done enough in the name of good sportsmanship."

She laughed, but then he was dancing them out, right across the ballroom floor in a sweeping, ridiculously romantic not-quite-a-waltz. She knew exactly how Cinderella felt, dancing on borrowed time.

The valet brought Declan's car around and she slid gratefully inside, leaning her head back against the buttery leather. A moment later, he joined her and got them on the road.

His right hand brushed her cheek briefly. "Come back with me?"

Her insides clenched. Her driver was one dead sexy man.

"Let's do my place," she said, needing the comfort of home and the familiar.

Tonight there were fewer paparazzi waiting out front, some of the furor over their dramatic capsizing and rescue having waned. They slipped past the photographers and Declan exchanged a few low words with Ryan before joining her inside her cottage. He looked large and very male in the small space.

Before she could forget, she pulled off the earrings and held them out to him. "You'd better take these back before I lose them, too."

He gave her a look. "They deserve a good home." He curled her fingers around the fistful of diamonds and rubies. "You keep them."

She groaned. She had no idea how much vintage Edwardian jewelry cost, but these earrings weren't roses or even a half dozen of Gitty's muffins. "I can't."

She set them carefully on the coffee table. Then she

kicked off her gorgeous sandals, groaning. "How can something so beautiful hurt so bad?"

"Absolutely no idea." His small half smile said that maybe he did know.

She hated to see him sad.

"We need a do-over on this week," she said, holding out her hands to him. "Dance with me."

He raised an eyebrow but he took her hands, mock-dancing her around the room while she hummed her favorite waltz. And if it might, just possibly, have starred a yellow dress and the prince of beasts, sue her. Everyone deserved a fantasy. Which reminded her...

She wound her arms around Declan's neck, tugging his face down to hers so she could breathe him in, then pressed her mouth to his where he tasted of champagne and something sweeter, wilder and all Declan. It turned out she had a serious Declan addiction.

"Are we still dancing?" he asked, but he wrapped his arms around her and swung her in one last, crazy slow circle. She tightened her grip on him but he set her on her feet, his hands sliding up her back and then down. He pulled her closer until she could feel the heat and strength of him through the tuxedo.

Which was bone-meltingly lovely, but not enough. She fisted the front of his dress shirt, dragging him nearer still. Her nipples tightened from the contact. "That's a no on the waltzing, but I have another idea, Hollywood."

"Found a use for Prince Charming after all?" he asked, voice hoarse, when they finally broke apart after another kiss.

"You bet. Think he takes orders?"

"He's willing to try. Always." He leaned into her, his lips finding hers again. "But he can be a screwup."

She rocked her hips against him, making him groan. "I hope there's a dirty pun in there."

He smiled. "I'm all yours."

"For right now."

His smile deepened. "It will always be right now."

"Good plan," she said breathlessly. "The absolute best of plans."

He nodded. "You want me to bring you your binder so you can immortalize it?"

"Declan." She ran her fingers along his jaw. "I'm pretty sure we sank that binder. Along with our boat."

The *Cupcake* had washed up on shore, so maybe someone had salvaged the binder, but she wasn't thinking straight, at least not about itemized plans and next steps. She blamed Declan for that. The heated look in his eyes didn't make her want to plan, or think about what would happen tomorrow or next. All she cared about was *right now*—and Declan.

"We'll figure it out," he promised hoarsely.

"Promise?"

And as if he'd read her mind, he made a very male sound and picked her up. Her cottage was so small that a few strides had them in her even tinier bedroom, a room that seemed a thousand times smaller now that it was full of Declan, or maybe that was just the too-big feelings squeezing her chest, her ribs, her heart…

"Yeah," he said. "Promise."

"So beautiful," Declan whispered, making short work of Charlotte's clothes and his own. This was his favorite side of her, the one that was bare and open, trusting him to make her feel good. And then when she made that cute little snort of disbelief that she made far too often, he gently placed his palm over her mouth. "The clothes and the fancy makeup are pretty, but they're like a picture frame for what I really want to look at. You don't need them, Char." His voice was whiskey-rough and strained as he rolled her on top of him, stroking her body with his hands as he drew sensual patterns over her skin.

"Don't lie to me," she said fiercely, straddling him. "Don't ever lie to me, not about this, not about us."

"Won't," he gritted out, running his hands up her soft thighs, tracing each curve with clever fingers. She was such a giver, so warm and open, her body heating for him where they touched, the rounded globes of her breasts meriting more kisses, the tight tips demanding his attention, and then his mouth explored the sun-kissed slopes and the paler skin that had been hidden beneath her swimsuit tops. She gasped out his name, her body welcoming him, moving restlessly as she gripped his shoulders and held on. It was…everything.

He lost himself in her, forgetting the race and where they were, the world camped outside this small, private place for the two of them. The brush of her skin on his sent pleasure shooting through him, her hands stroking him, her mouth pressing kisses against his throat, his shoulder. He loved that she trusted him to give her this, heat and desire racing through his body as she touched him and he loved each part of her that he could.

"Charlotte."

She stared down at him, dazed. "We really don't need to have a conversation right now."

"Is this okay?"

He gripped her hips gently, his thumbs stroking over the sensitive skin and moving down to where she was slick and wet.

"Don't you dare stop," she whispered. And then, "Please, Declan."

She leaned down into him and he kissed her, his fingers never stopping until the rhythm of her breathing changed, her body tensing. He found a condom and then he was inside her, guiding her hips in a new, harder rhythm that made them both groan, half words and rough pleas falling from their mouths.

Their next kiss wasn't as sweet as their last kiss had been. It was hungry and open, things Declan usually didn't share with anyone because he hated being vulnerable. But Charlotte cupped his face with her hands, her breath coming in short gasps as she kissed him back, her hips rocking on him, and if she could do it, he wanted to as well. She was trusting and open, sweet and so goddamned giving that he just *knew*. No matter what happened with Masterson Entertainment, with his father and the work projects he'd thought mattered so much, he'd already won when this woman chose him to make love to her—to be her partner in every sense of the word.

Her face pressed against his throat even as she let out a few of the sexiest whimpers he'd ever heard. "Can you finish this, please?" she asked, sounding desperate. "Now, Declan. Right now. Please."

So he did, giving her what they both needed because he was hers right now and, quite possibly, forever.

Seventeen

The day was shaping up to be a Martha's Vineyard classic, full of sunshine and bright blue sky. The weather had been picture-perfect in the two weeks since the race, as if to make things up to her. Unfortunately, even if Charlotte had had a free minute to step outside and enjoy it, paparazzi had parked across the street from Martha's Kids. Earlier today, when she'd stepped outside with her PB&J, hoping to eat down by the water, they'd pounced. Ryan had convinced them to back off, but lesson learned. Free time now meant inside time. Preferably in-bed time.

With Declan.

She loved the time they spent in bed. A lot. Declan was always in motion, running, racing, putting his body through its paces because the man loved challenges. And even though the Vineyard got its share of famous visitors, the summer tourists stared when they were out and about, asking to take selfies with him or for an autograph. Public Declan was charming, but the private man was hers alone. He laughed easily, his eyes full of warmth as he sprawled like the king of the cats, listening to her talk. Nothing threw him. He was calm, sure of the next step to take but careful not to force his opinions on her. And the way he was always touching her... She loved that, too. He'd sling an arm around her, give her shoulder a gentle squeeze when he came back into a room where she was and stroke her hair. She'd never been a touchy-feely person but she loved how he touched her. Her face flushed as she remembered just how much she loved it. They'd kept each other up far too late last night.

Five minutes ago, she'd been looking forward to the end of a long day trying to make their nonexistent budget work when she'd got a phone call from the district attorney's office. Never, she reminded herself, make the mistake of thinking a day couldn't get worse.

Because it could.

The district attorney's office had what they needed to press charges against George Moore even if they hadn't yet found the bastard. It had been a lengthy process. She'd turned over copies of the foundation's bookkeeping records and then had made herself available to answer their questions. Finally, the DA had *sufficient evidence to take to a grand jury.* She'd known for months, of course, that George was a lying, stealing weasel, but now it would officially be public knowledge. She no longer needed to keep silent and there would be an epic PR storm when the news broke.

She wasn't sure what to do next, which was a first. She always had a plan and finishing the letter of resignation that she'd drafted when she'd first realized what George had done seemed like it should be number one on her to-do list. It was just that she'd stupidly thought she'd have more time, that she could find a solution to the damage. Instead, she'd failed. She suspected that failure was about to make it onto national television thanks to her not-so-fake-now relationship with Declan.

A tap on her office door had her looking up. Declan stood there, sun-bronzed and relaxed. Her heart skipped a beat.

After the crazy finish to their race, they'd done round after round of media interviews. There had been photographs and invitations to appear on several television programs, all of which she'd begged off. He'd done them, though, and she'd watched, marveling at his ease in front of the cameras. And at that thought, she winced a little. Despite his makeover lessons and the designer clothes, she was still Charlotte. She didn't fit into his Hollywood lifestyle and couldn't imagine life lived in that fishbowl. And she'd tried—because this thing between her and Declan wasn't just sex or even the friendship that she'd come to value so highly. It was both of those things, as well as the fact that her heart had gotten involved as well and the end of the summer was coming closer and closer.

Today was the first time since the winners' banquet that Declan hadn't had a scheduled appearance and she'd planned to catch up on work before heading out to watch the fireworks at Oak Bluffs with him. It had been his idea that they go out tonight and she didn't have the heart to tell him that she would have preferred to spend it alone with him rather than in a crowd. She didn't know when he had to head back to Hollywood and his film studio, but she doubted they had much more time together and she didn't want to waste it in public. Her heart seized at the relaxed smile playing around the corners of his mouth.

"Are you okay?"

"A bad phone call," she said. "But nothing unexpected."

He leaned down, capturing her mouth in a kiss. Because she'd driven to work, he followed her back to her place in his car. And then, when he followed her inside and she tried to get changed because she wasn't watching fireworks in business casual, thank you very much, one thing led to another and it was close to sunset before they got out of bed and on the road.

The fireworks at Oak Bluffs were legendary and the night was clear and perfect. Visitors and year-round residents crowded the grassy expanse, picnicking around a white bandstand lit up and decorated in bunting. A brass band cranked out Sousa tunes. Declan grabbed their supplies from his car and then threaded his fingers through hers, drawing her through the crowd and to the bandstand.

Proving he got her more than anyone else ever had, he'd stocked their picnic basket with lobster rolls and root beer in glass bottles. And true to form, they'd started their picnic with dessert first: cupcakes from Gitty's bakery truck. Afterward, he tugged her onto his lap. Fortunately it was growing dark, although she spotted at least one cell phone turned their way. Maybe she'd get lucky and a former president or a rap star would show up.

As the band wrapped up their next-to-last number,

he shifted her off his lap. "I need you to do something for me." He smiled at her. "Think you can do that?"

She had some very pleasurable memories of the last time he'd ask that particular question. "Does it involve my holding very, very still while you have your wicked way with me? Because there are far too many people here for that to work. Only one of us is comfortable with performing in public."

He groaned. "You're killing me. And no. Not yet. Give me five minutes more here and remember that I love you."

She still got a fizzing sensation when he said those three words to her. It was surreal. More than once over the past year she'd wondered, mostly when she'd been hiding in her bed, what was so wrong with her that no one stuck around. Her father hadn't noticed when she disappeared. The man she thought she'd loved and had promised to marry had seen her as a means to money. No one had wanted her for *her*. No one had wanted to stay. She'd promised herself she wouldn't whine and that she'd get on with her life—and then Declan had crashed into it.

"I love you right back," she said.

He dropped a quick kiss on her mouth and then stood, tugging her up with him. "That's a promise. Don't forget."

The music stopped and then the band started again, but it wasn't the usual 1812 Overture that always ended the fireworks show. Train's "Marry Me" filled the air as Declan dropped to one knee in front of her, smiling up into her eyes. "Will you?"

She had no idea what script he was reading from or what her line was. There was a roaring sound in her ears, a foggy sensation creeping over her. Her face flushed as everyone around them turned to watch them.

"What?"

"Marry me." He wrapped his fingers around hers. "Charlotte, will you marry me?"

She smiled back automatically. This was… *Yes*, her heart screamed. Her brain thought… Well, it had derailed because the last month had been amazing, maybe the best of her life. Declan was a great guy who believed in her and who'd stuck with her through some hard moments. She was working, trying to make a difference for her foster kids, and for the first time in what felt like forever she was one-hundred-percent in charge of her own life…except for those late-night visits with Declan, because the man was deliciously bossy in bed and made the best suggestions about how he could please her.

That was amazing.

It was love.

A game changer.

She didn't know what this was, although it sure seemed like the game had changed. Again.

People around them were whispering, a sea of cell phones capturing their moment. *Did she say yes yet? Did he get down on one knee? Can you see the ring?*

She stared back at them, suddenly wishing she was anywhere else, and realized her teammates from Martha's Kids were in the crowd. None of them had mentioned that *they* were planning on attending tonight's fireworks. And there was…her father? Now that she looked, the entire Vineyard seemed to have packed itself onto the lawn—and none of them were watching the sky for fireworks.

They were all staring at Charlotte and Declan.

Declan, who was holding out a small, open velvet box with the hand that wasn't wrapped around hers.

She reached for it automatically. It was a diamond ring, an absolutely beautiful ring. A gift and a promise. The kind of sparkle that all the best dreams had.

"Say yes?" her dream man asked, looking up at her.

Her mouth wanted to blurt out "yes" and get right on with the business of happily ever after, while her heart helpfully offered a list of all the reasons that was the best-ever plan. One: he was so strong and sure of himself. Two: he fought for what he believed in and she loved that that included her. Three: he kept his promises and he didn't let go. Or was that four? And five... He was a charmer who had fought his way to the top and who now wanted to share his life with her. He gently rubbed her fingers, waiting patiently.

"Declan," she whispered. A camera shutter clicked somewhere.

"I love you," he said, his eyes serious. "Marry me. Yes?"

She nodded. He slid the ring on to her finger.

The crowd whooped and the band burst into a new song, an ad-hoc wedding march. She'd had no idea a brass band could do that.

Fireworks exploded overhead spelling out: SHE SAID... YES.

At least someone had added the ellipsis, as if there had been a chance she would say no. Would they have sky-written a refusal? She choked back a hysterical giggle, but Declan was on his feet, wrapping his arms around her and swinging her in a dizzying circle as he whooped. All he had time to do was plant a brief, hot kiss on her mouth before their audience moved in to congratulate them.

Later, after they'd spoken with what had to be almost every person on the island, she found herself face-to-face with J.J., Declan's father. He fit easily into the Vineyard's celebrity crowd with his expensive haircut and tailored pants, his white dress shirt rolled up to reveal tanned forearms. Money was just the polish, she realized, as he held out his hands to her. The man radiated power and authority, a confidence stemming from years as a Hollywood power player.

"Welcome to the family." He pulled her in for a brief hug.

Charlotte wasn't a fan of casual hugging with people she didn't know well, but it was easier to embrace him quickly and then step back than to refuse. She'd have a lifetime to get to know him. Her heart started beating hard and fast again, pounding out an *oh God, oh God, oh God* rhythm with each frantic pulse.

"You're absolutely perfect," her future father-in-law announced. "I approve." She didn't think he was looking for her agreement, so she smiled and leaned into Declan, not sure what to think. Perfection wasn't her strongest selling point.

"Well, thank God for your approval," Declan said dryly.

"You chose the better prize," his father continued. "Sure, you lost the boat race and we'll get around to discussing that later, but this lady right here? She's everything I'd expect from a Masterson bride-to-be."

Charlotte had no idea what he was trying to convey to Declan. What, exactly, was she perfect *for*? She felt as if she'd stumbled into a conversation that had started long before she'd arrived. Maybe Declan's dad was just weird or lived in the nineteenth century when parental approval was actually a thing. Maybe J.J. needed to feel like he was the center of attention. She didn't need to have the conversation now, not when she was getting married—*married*—to the man she loved. Suddenly the whole evening was too overwhelming.

"Can we get out of here?" she asked Declan, leaning more heavily on him.

"Anything you want," he said firmly, the smile fading from his face. "Always."

Eighteen

The large, decadently chocolate muffin on Charlotte's desk looked lonely. It needed a muffin best friend or two—or possibly a cast of friends like a TV sitcom, because she planned to eat her sorrows. She held her hand out. "Muffin me."

A new muffin landed in her outstretched hand. Bran, from the grainy texture. "Are you kidding me?"

"Friends don't let friends muffin alone," Gitty said. "Plus, there's only one chocolate muffin left and my day has sucked."

Gitty gave her a small smile. Brown curls bobbing, gray eyes warm with sympathy, she waved a plastic knife at the chocolate muffin she held in her other hand. "But I'm willing to be convinced to go halfsies if it's an emergency."

Uh-oh. Sharing—the sad details of her day or the muffin—was not part of today's plan.

"Waiting for a life update," Gitty prompted.

Charlotte took a bite of muffin. Unfortunately, no amount of delicious sugar and chocolate chips could help her. "There are reporters outside. I'm never leaving the building again."

"Like one of those medieval nuns who live in a cloister?"

Charlotte had no idea if it was a thing or not, but it sounded good to her. "I'm going to give it my best shot. I'm pretty sure you can get everything delivered these days."

"You may need to dig a moat," Gitty offered. "There are a lot of reporters. Also, they like muffins and I charged them double."

Timma, the Martha's Kids' staffer who had volunteered to do reconnaissance behind enemy lines, popped her head in the door, knocking on the frame as she did so. "Six reporters out front."

"Crap," Charlotte said. "Okay. Company meeting in here, please."

Three minutes later, she, Gitty and the three staff members were crammed into her tiny office.

"Why are there reporters out front?" Thea asked. Barely five feet tall, fifty-something Thea ran their office like a benevolent dictator. Not only was she a spreadsheet whiz, but she always crocheted something for each office birthday. She also had an uncanny knack for ferreting out secrets.

Charlotte looked at her.

"Okay, so we all know," Thea admitted. "But we figured you'd rather tell us and we'd rather to hear the George details from you anyhow. Go straight to the source."

Charlotte fiddled with her muffin and tried not to angry cry. Timma reached over and stole a bite of muffin.

"George didn't quit," she said. "He emptied my bank account, then he emptied Martha's Kids'. Our summer camp budget is currently ten dollars. We're broke because of the chief financial officer I hired. I'd hoped that the charity boat race would refill our coffers. I failed you all and I'm deeply sorry." *Hope is not a strategy*, her father's voice announced in her head. *Thanks, Dad. I'm aware of that.*

Timma choked on the muffin. Thea cursed. And Mimi just looked like she might be plotting murder. Charlotte had never loved them more.

Gitty raised her hand. "Do you think George came here deliberately to meet you?"

What did it say about her that that hadn't occurred to her? She'd just assumed he'd romanced her to gain her trust after realizing she was the director. "So my entire relationship was a hunting expedition?"

"I think you should consider the possibility." Gitty handed Charlotte another muffin. "Banana chocolate chip, so it counts as a serving of fruit."

Gitty had a wide-eyed look of wholesomeness that was totally at odds with her lack of a filter and boisterous enthusiasm for life. Gitty didn't stop at one muffin if she was still hungry and wanted a second, and during their middle school days she'd taught Charlotte how to drink out of a glass soda bottle without getting her tongue stuck, shared her hot pockets and called out the playground bully, who had decided Charlotte's old-fashioned name begged for some ugly nicknames.

"So what happens now?" Thea asked.

"I don't know exactly," Charlotte said honestly. "But I'm on it. I'll keep you all in the loop. I do know that the district attorney is filing charges and law enforcement is officially looking for George so they can arrest him."

Timma frowned. "Will he have to give back the money?"

"If he still has it, yes." Charlotte paused. "But I'm guessing he didn't take it just to have it."

That was the cue for everyone to start talking at once, discussing George's potential shopping list. Thea voted for real estate because every evil villain needed a private, gated estate, while Timma wondered if he'd invested in cryptocurrency. Gitty was sure he must have a secret gambling problem.

Charlotte knew he had a character problem.

She, on the other hand, had a PR problem. After Charlotte's team had left, with Charlotte's repeated promises that she was doing everything she could to fix the problem and that their jobs were secure, she and Gitty scrolled through the social media postings. The big Hollywood gossip sites had run the story about how the famous movie star's brand-new fiancée was facing a career-ending audit as to why and how her previous fiancé had run off with almost a million dollars. There were the not-unexpected speculations: that Charlotte was in on it and just waiting for her chance to relocate to Belize or Fiji; that a brokenhearted Declan had fled to his Hollywood mansion and the arms of not one but three of his former costars; that he'd broken it off between Charlotte and him because loving her plain-Jane self was a clever PR move to whitewash his dented reputation.

"So you broke up with George—and congratulations

on that, by the way," Gitty said. "And then you upgraded and dated a movie star."

"George left me," she pointed out.

"Details. You would have dumped him when you confirmed he was an ethics-less asshole. But since you didn't tell your team here about George's actions, I have to ask. Did you tell Declan? Or is he finding out right now?"

Charlotte looked out of the window to where Gitty was pointing and tried not to panic. Because she was right. Declan had just pulled up and the reporters were all over him—and no, she hadn't told him. She'd wanted to fix her mess before confessing.

"I just found out two months ago and then I had a chance to make up the shortfall if I won the charity boat race and I took it."

"So that's a *no* on sharing with him." Gitty patted her hand. "But honey, the thing is—people share with their friends. Their family. The ones they love. And if Declan is all of that for you, why couldn't you tell him?"

Someone knocked on the door, saving her from yet another non-confession.

"I'd bet the last muffin that's your Prince Charming rushing to the rescue," Gitty said and nudged her. "I'd recommend letting him in."

Since that seemed like as good a plan as any, Charlotte got up and went to the front door to let Declan in. He didn't look happy.

"Why didn't you call me?" he asked.

Charlotte had no idea where to start, but Gitty didn't have that problem.

Staring intently at her phone, she said, "Because she

was busy freaking out. And also, isn't this at least fifty percent your fault?"

Charlotte had no idea what Gitty was talking about, but she appreciated the support. Mostly. She did not, however, want an audience for this conversation with Declan.

Ignoring Gitty, Declan met her gaze. "I'm not George Moore."

"Neither is she," Gitty said, undeterred.

Charlotte froze and tried to get her mouth to work. She had to say something because this was her conversation to have, her and Declan. It didn't matter how much she hated confrontation or confession, particularly when she was the one in the wrong.

Gitty didn't look up from her phone, but she didn't hold back, either. "Uh-huh. You had to know this was coming. You let those people out here get their morning-after pictures. You let Charlotte walk into this. No one would be staking out the parking lot if you weren't a freaking Hollywood star."

"If I'd known that embezzlement charges were about to come out, I would have handled this differently."

"Right," said Gitty slowly. "But would you have skipped the proposal altogether?"

Declan and Charlotte both turned to stare at her. "What?"

Gitty held out her phone. Charlotte took it, heart sinking as she scrolled down the screen. Unflattering morning-after pictures of her post–boat wreck? Check. Additional morning-after picture of her not so sneakily leaving Declan's place? Check. Pictures of him leaving *her* place? Yep. Worse than the speculation about their sex life, though, was the newest headline.

Hollywood Bad Boy Signs Good Guy Contract?

She had to read the story twice before the truth started to sink in. According to "reliable sources," Declan had made a deal with J.J., a bargain where he traded his good behavior and rehabilitated public image for the family film company. The gossip site suggested that the well-timed, highly public proposal to a wholesome, plain-Jane local girl had been intended to seal that deal and paper over a night of debauched, post-wreck sex. *You chose the better prize,* J.J.'s voice echoed in her head. *She's everything I'd expect from a Masterson bride-to-be.*

She put the phone down and looked at Declan, who said the three words that killed a relationship faster than anything.

"I can explain," he said.

She really wished he would.

He'd said she was perfect, but maybe she should have asked him for a list of reasons why. Hurt twisted her stomach into a hard knot and slammed her stupid, hopeful heart into her ribs as tears smarted her eyes.

"These are angry tears," she told him. "I cry when I'm mad."

"Charlotte, look at me."

She did, because apparently she *could* make a greater fool out of herself. He met her gaze, the expression on his face pitying.

"Oh my God," she said. "It's all true, isn't it?"

"For fuck's sake," he growled. "You can't think I proposed to get a film studio."

"That would be a dowry first," Gitty said. She stood up, grabbed her phone and headed toward the door. "Right. I'm leaving now."

Charlotte waited until she was sure that Gitty had let herself out and the door had closed behind her. Given the way her life was going, she didn't want to risk a reporter sneaking in and accidentally-on-purpose overhearing their conversation.

"Did you actually have a contract with your dad about inheriting Masterson Entertainment?" The media lied. Exaggerated. She knew that.

He scrubbed a hand over his head. "Yes, J.J. and I had a deal in place before I came to Martha's Vineyard. You don't have to worry about it. It's over and done with and it was between him and me."

"We did this too fast." She felt numb, which was probably a good thing. "The engagement was a mistake."

We were a mistake.

He wasn't who he'd said he was. Or rather, his reasons for pursuing her weren't what he'd claimed. She'd thought he wanted her for herself, but instead she'd been a means of sealing a deal with his father.

"Charlotte, please listen to me."

"Maybe you should tell me what you were thinking. Why this made sense to you."

She grabbed her tote bag and started shoving things into it. Her laptop. A random stack of papers from the desktop. The muffins.

"You were never window dressing, Charlotte."

On that point, she agreed with him. "Well I don't look like window dressing, now do I?"

Or wait, maybe she did? She scrolled through the article again. A *good guy* contract. J.J. had made it perfectly clear—in writing, no less—that Declan needed to rehabilitate his public image. And what better way to do that than by falling in love and serving up a fairy-tale wedding? She wasn't going to do this a second time.

She yanked at his ring on her finger. "Take this back."

"I can explain," he said again.

Handsome, charming George hadn't bothered with explanations. He had been, she'd realized too late, the center of his own world and she'd merely been a useful appliance, propping up his public image and making it easier for him to do whatever he wanted. And while Declan had only stolen her heart, she couldn't do it again. She wouldn't be the window dressing for someone else's life so that that someone else could live his dream life.

She held out the ring. "I won't live in a fishbowl and I won't be a convenient choice."

Declan locked eyes with her. "Believe me, there's nothing convenient about you. Talk to me."

That hurt. "I won't be the cheat sheet on your inheritance test."

"So that's it? One piece of bad press and you're done with us?"

"No," she said. "One hard piece of truth and I'm done with us. It's not what they wrote, although it hurt to read. It's that it's the truth, Declan. You made a deal with your dad and you never shared that with me. You had so many chances to say, 'Hey, my old man will turn over the family company to me if I turn over a new leaf.' You should have told me."

"And you should have told me about George, about the problems at Martha's Kids."

She set the ring down on the desk. "I didn't want you to think I was anything less than perfect."

"Right," he said. "How's that working out for you? Ready to admit that you need help and to let someone get close to you?"

She looked at him. "If I am, that someone won't be you."

Then she turned and walked out of the room.

Nineteen

Don't let someone who isn't worth your love make you forget how much you're worth.

If he can walk away from you, let him walk.

Forget what's gone.

Or who.

Charlotte glared at her phone. She'd discovered in a late-night, ice-cream-fueled binge internet session that Declan was back in California and that people actually made breakup apps. Since anti-dating seemed like a smart plan, she'd downloaded one that flooded her screen with inspirational quotes at suspiciously opportune moments, as if it could telepathically sense her weakness, which would have been a neat trick for a bunch of bits and bytes or whatever it was software apps were made of.

Of course, *she* was the one who'd done the breaking

up—at least, the hostile-word-exchange part—but still. She was *broken up*, if that was a word. Or a thing. The ache in her chest whenever she thought about Declan was painful. She prodded at it like a sore tooth, trying to see if everything was miraculously better. And… Nope.

Declan had still come to Martha's Vineyard fully intending to swap a race win for a CEO and owner role at Masterson Entertainment. If he'd been up-front about what he had riding on the race outcome, she'd have done things differently—or at least been better prepared and less shocked.

You weren't one-hundred-percent honest either, were you?

She shoved her phone into her desk drawer and shifted her glare to her laptop screen where she'd just finished revising her resignation letter. And then she hit the Send button.

Two seconds later Thea barreled into her office. Wow. Even for Thea, that was fast. "What did you do?"

"I resigned," she said. "I'm sorry. What I did just isn't fixable."

"You're just going to leave us?" Thea wanted to know.

"I let down our kids. I don't deserve to stay."

The ache in her chest got worse. Her head, clearly jealous of the attention, decided to throb along. Ignoring Thea's protestation, she grabbed her box of things and went outside. Now that the paparazzi had given up on her and Declan, she could walk unimpeded to her car. Her Kate Middleton moment was over. She could go to the grocery store in her pajamas and only the cashier and her fellow shoppers would know—not random people in North Dakota or Timbuktu. She'd made the mistake of reading the online comments once and people were harsh when they didn't say it to your face.

The sound of someone laying on a horn drew Charlotte's attention across the street. Right. It was Monday, so it was Muffin Monday and that meant Gitty's bakery truck. At one o'clock in the afternoon, the breakfast pastry crowd had dwindled and the afternoon cookie line hadn't yet formed.

"Did someone die?" Gitty yelled.

She shoved the box of crap into her car and marched across the street. "Do you think I have a problem asking people for help?"

"Do you want an honest answer or are you going to shoot the messenger?"

Charlotte narrowed her eyes. "Okay. So I'm hearing a *yes*. Except why won't you just come out and say it?"

Gitty sighed. "I promised I'd work on my filter, but what the heck. I'll start tomorrow. You hate asking for help. Remember when you got trapped in the bathroom in the fourth grade and you wouldn't admit it for hours? We all thought you had food poisoning but you were trying and failing to figure out how to take the door off its hinges."

"I'm sorry. I could—"

"Don't say 'fix it,'" Gitty said softly. "You don't have to fix everything. You can't—no one could—and as your friend, I'm not okay with what that does to you."

"I can't fix this," she admitted. "No matter how much I want to. Martha's Kids is out of money. We can't fund the summer camps. Raising those funds was my responsibility, so I've resigned."

Gitty nodded. "And did you ask the board what they

thought was best for Martha's Kids? Maybe you could try asking them for help?"

She hadn't. She thought about that while Gitty made her a coffee and popped a leftover muffin into a paper bag for her. She'd tried to handle everything on her own. She'd insisted on it, because if you fixed the thing fast enough, you didn't even have to confess that you'd been the one to break it in the first place.

"I should have brought the budget issues to their attention," she admitted.

Gitty nodded. "And?"

"And—" She stopped because, really, she didn't know what the next step was. She looked at Gitty, who also shrugged.

"And then there would have been a bunch of smart, caring people brainstorming solutions," Gitty said. "And maybe one would have worked. Maybe you would still be broke. But there would have been an apology followed by a conversation."

There probably would also have been yelling, finger-pointing and…forgiveness.

"I made another mistake, but this one I can fix." She had to un-quit.

Gitty flashed her a thumbs-up. "You've got this."

Charlotte wasn't as sure, but she was going to try. Oh, boy. She was going to try. Turning around, she marched back inside Martha's Kids and into her former office. Hopefully still her office, she told herself. And then she fired off a second email, taking back the first one, since as they ran a summer camp and not a multi-national IT company, no one had figured out yet how to shut down her email or change the locks.

"We have a budget problem," she told Thea when

Thea stuck her head in the door a few minutes later. "And could you schedule a board meeting for as soon as possible? I need to explain the situation to them and pitch some possible solutions." She sucked in a breath and looked at Thea. "But I need help to do that. I need your help."

Thea smiled. "On it, boss lady."

Charlotte knocked on the front door of the house, keeping a wary eye on the bushes and driveway. No paparazzi jumped out to snap her, which she put in the *win* column. She could only imagine the stories they'd have spun. She didn't miss the unwelcome attention. But she did miss…

Declan.

She was done with pretending to be perfect, pretending that she had her shit together and that she took full responsibility for what she got wrong. She just wanted to let go.

And go to Declan.

Her father actually opened his own front door. He looked around the driveway, then turned and walked into the house. She followed him to his study.

"You moved out," he said, sitting down behind the big desk. He had the same look on his face that he'd had when the election results came in and his candidate had lost.

She had. Turned out, it was hard to draw boundaries with her father when she walked past him every day. "I did."

"So now you'll pay rent when you're lucky to still have a job at all. You got it all wrong there, Charlotte. You didn't have the experience or the charisma to handle a man like George Moore. He rolled you and your board."

The zing of shame in her stomach was familiar. Ignoring it was not, but she tried. "I didn't," she admitted. "I—"

But her father was on a roll. "You're too trusting. Naive. You had a good thing with that actor and then what happened? He made you look like a fool, too."

"George did that stuff," she said even though he was still talking and not listening. "Not me. I interviewed him. I voted to hire him. Clearly I did not make sure we had a good process in place or he wouldn't have been able to make off with the money he did. And yeah, he cleaned me out, too. I trusted him. That was my mistake. But I'm not responsible for his stealing or for his leaving because he was too much of a cowardly shit to own up to his mistakes."

It was a good speech, one she might have practiced before coming over, but it was wasted. Her father talked over the whole thing, commenting on Declan's shortcomings and her failure to keep him in line. "You were looking better. Today you're windblown and your nose is red. I don't understand why you can't make an effort. It's not that hard."

Translation: her makeover had worn off, although she'd kept the cashmere.

"I've done what I could to help you," her father continued. "You wanted to participate in this race and I got you a partner who all but guaranteed a win: handsome, athletic, knew how to win a crowd and how to sail a boat. You could have taken Martha's Kids to the next level with the prize."

"You picked Declan as my partner," she said numbly. "I thought it was random."

"His father owed me a favor," he said. "I made a quick call, reminded him of that."

It was nice that her father had wanted her to win. Except that he'd wanted her to win because he thought she was a failure at her job. He thought she needed to *take Martha's Kids to the next level* despite her repeated explanations that the organization's size was a choice and not a mistake. Like he always had, he'd ignored her.

"I have to go," she said. "No, I want to go. I've said what I needed to and this isn't a conversation. This is you telling me—*again*—that I've disappointed you. I know that, but it's going to have to be okay because I can't fix it. I *won't* fix it. Oh and FYI, I'm canceling on our next lunch date."

As her father blustered on, she left the room.

This wasn't a movie. There wasn't a script and a next line. Declan had said she refused to let other people help, that she insisted on fixing things that weren't her mistakes. He'd been right. She couldn't do this on her own. Fixing what wasn't right in her foster kids' lives would take more than one person, no matter how much that person cared. It took a team. An island's worth.

Declan had also said that he held on when he had to, even when it was hard and it hurt and letting go would have been the safer option.

She'd done the opposite.

She'd let go.

Of him, of her life, of the things she couldn't control. And instead she'd held on far too tightly to all the wrong things: The pride that had her hating to ask for help. The ugliness of her father's emotional abuse. The hurtfulness of George's betrayal.

It hurt her, holding on so tightly. She opened the front door and went outside. It would be nice if she could let go of all of those things that were so bad for her as easily as she'd stepped over her father's threshold, but she had to accept that it wouldn't be easy. She'd have to do it one step at a time and sometimes she might go backward instead of forward. She'd watched Declan throw himself into life, the race, their relationship, willing to take the risk even if it meant possibly crash-landing. He'd given it everything.

While she'd held back, afraid of losing.

Twenty

Declan had jumped off buildings and bridges. He'd launched himself from planes and mountainsides with explosions licking at his heels. It wasn't all that often that he hesitated and he'd built a reputation in Hollywood for his ability to do whatever it took to make a scene happen. Even when Charlotte had disappeared over the side of the *Cupcake*, he'd known exactly what to do next: follow her, hold onto her, bring her safely to shore. Being strong enough, fast enough, well-trained enough—that had been, well, *enough*.

Now he had no clue what came next.

His agent was still angry about the quickie engagement and breakup. He'd been rooting for the perfect fairy-tale ending to Declan and Charlotte's story and then Charlotte had returned his ring. Hell, she'd kicked him out without considering the optics or what people would say. She'd called him out for making their relationship be about other people and for putting his career first—for that goddamned stupid contract he'd signed with J.J., which hadn't been about being his own boss or being the CEO of a successful company. Part of him was still the kid who'd been left in the foster care system by his parents and then adopted. And adopted meant that someone could take it back. Could take his life away and tell him to go.

Bottom line? He was afraid of being left so he made sure he was the one who left first, and if he couldn't do that? He made a game out of the relationship he'd been seeking, so it was all fun and nothing that could actually hurt him.

He'd thought he'd be fine, that he'd get over his feelings for Charlotte, that he'd go back to California and immerse himself in Masterson Entertainment and everything would be fine.

He wasn't fine. The media coverage after their breakup had been as bad as his publicist had predicted. Articles had speculated about his relationship with Charlotte. Nothing nice had been said and the pictures had been worse. All sorts of people had also come forward, too, from previously unknown members of the biological family to Vineyard residents who, it turned out, had plenty to say about Charlotte and her ex-fiancé.

And then there had been today's new development: a picture of George being escorted off a plane from the Bahamas in handcuffs. From what he'd heard, Charlotte's ex wanted to make a deal to avoid the consequences of his actions as much as possible and had shared in great detail what he'd done at Martha's Kids and how. The *how* concentrated on Charlotte's gullibility and her falling for George's charm, which turned her big heart and openness to trusting people into a fatal flaw rather than further evidence that she was an amazing person.

What pissed Declan off most, however, was that the impending demise of Martha's Kids was a footnote in the media coverage. The disappointed kids who wouldn't get their summer camp experience, the people in Charlotte's office who counted on their paycheck from the foundation, all of Charlotte's plans—those were collateral damage. Since that was just about the only thing he could fix, he'd made an anonymous donation yesterday.

But that was just money, which he had plenty of. He was across the fucking country from her when he needed to be there by her side. Or, since she'd sent him away in no uncertain terms, he needed to be on the island. Down the street. Anywhere he could do something for her. If George made her cry or worry one second more than he already had, Declan had plans of his own and he was implementing step one today.

He'd made the journey from his Santa Monica house to Hollywood in record time. They had two films in postproduction and a new shoot starting on-site this week for one of his particular projects, so there should have been questions aimed his way. Most of the people on the lot, however, detoured out of his way once they got a good look at him. He knew he looked grim as he stormed inside.

"J.J.?" he demanded of the young guy parked at the receptionist's desk.

"Conference room. I'll let him know you're here, Mr. Masterson." The receptionist stood up, discreetly trying to block Declan's path, but Declan was around him and down the hall before he'd finished speaking.

He'd spent plenty of time in that conference room. He'd hammered out contracts, argued the pros and cons of projects and fought for Masterson Entertainment repeatedly. Today J.J. sat in his usual spot at the head of the long table. He didn't look surprised to see Declan, although Nash's presence on his right-hand side was unexpected. Nash didn't often leave his chemistry lab, even though he'd already earned a fortune from his research. He nodded at his brother, who nodded back.

J.J. said nothing.

Classic power move.

Declan didn't know what he'd hoped his adoptive father would say, but it wouldn't have been the kind of stuff movie fathers said about how they were proud no matter what the kid did. J.J. prized winning. And sure enough, that was where the man started when he decided the silence had stretched on long enough.

"You lost," J.J. said, not bothering with a greeting. "Sell me on why I should still make you my heir and not take the buyout offer I have."

Nash leaned forward like a hunting dog scenting his target. "So the media coverage is actually true? You were stupid enough to sign a contract with him?"

He reminded himself that he loved his brother. "I was, but that's not on today's agenda."

Nash gave him a level look. "Are there slides for this agenda? Speaker notes? I was told this was a family lunch and I'm feeling unprepared."

J.J. cleared his throat and they both looked at him. Declan had been on the receiving end of J.J.'s disapproving looks before, but this was the last time. He might be an ass, but he wasn't too proud to learn from the smart people in his life. Charlotte had made the decision to stand up for what she believed in. She'd put her shoulders back and walked into a ballroom as if she were royalty and that woman hadn't been half as brave as the woman who'd told him to get lost. She made him want to be a better man. Well, that and she just made his world better.

"Declan did sign a contract with me," J.J. said for Nash's benefit. "We made a deal. He'd get Masterson Entertainment if he could prove that he was Masterson material."

"You gave him an inheritance test," Nash scowled. He didn't seem to mind that he hadn't been invited to take the test or that J.J. had effectively disinherited him.

"You did rehabilitate your image some," J.J. said to Declan, ignoring Nash entirely. As if what Declan cared about was how people talked about him. There was only one person who mattered. Okay. Two. Nash—and now Charlotte. "Getting yourself engaged to a genuine New England princess was clever, although you seem to have lost yet another fiancée."

"Asking Charlotte to marry me was the smartest thing I've ever done," he interrupted. "And she's a god-damned queen."

"Have you told her that?" Nash asked.

Declan hadn't. And since that was *also* something he could fix, he pulled out his phone and texted Charlotte. I'm an ass and I miss you. He hadn't stared at his phone waiting for a woman to respond since, well, ever, so this was a first for him. And while he hadn't really expected a handful of words to magically fix everything he'd screwed up, he was still disappointed when she didn't text him back.

He held up a palm when J.J. opened his mouth and started to talk. There was nothing he could say that mattered. "We need to get a couple of things straight. First, I'm done here. I quit. No more tests. I'm starting my own film studio, so heads up that Masterson Entertainment has a new competitor and we intend to kick your ass. Second…" He shook his head. "No, wait. That covers it. I'm out."

Then he turned around and got himself the hell away from J.J. No more contests, no more manipulation. Probably shouldn't have thrown down the gauntlet quite so obviously at J.J., but he was trying to change, not become a completely different person. He was competitive; he went after what he wanted. And even though he had more money than one man could spend thanks to his career, he couldn't sit around doing nothing. And that included doing nothing about Charlotte. He needed her back.

But after the very public nature of their courtship on Martha's Vineyard, he knew he needed to be cautious. Charlotte hated being the center of attention, although he hoped to convince her that she might like being the center of one particular person's attention. His.

Nash followed him out of the conference room, catching up with him as he entered the stairwell. "What were you thinking back there?"

He took the stairs two at a time. "I thought it was clear. If J.J. still wants a Masterson to run the family company, you can be the new CEO and future owner. Or he can hunt down Revere. I'll send a congratulatory fruit basket if that makes things clearer."

His brother grimaced. Of course, that was pretty much Nash's resting face. Nash was grumpy, surly and watched Declan's back with the ferocity of a dragon, albeit a very well-dressed, very wealthy dragon. "You're really going to walk away from all this because of Charlotte."

"Yeah." Declan shoved the door at the bottom of the stairwell open and headed for the front door. People spotted the two of them and rethought approaching them. Thunder and lightning. That's what people called them. Nash was the large, dark and glowering brother, while he was the brighter, hotter brother.

"Holy shit," his brother said. "You really do love her."

"I do." He leveled a look at his brother.

Who wasn't deterred.

Nash sped up and got to Declan's car first, crossing his arms over his chest as he leaned back on it. "So you went to sail in this big charity race because J.J. was all hot about the Jessie St. Chiles thing. I'm not sure why you thought proposing bare-ass naked and with a dollar's worth of fake bling was going to work, but that's a problem for a different day. So you go, you race, you partner with Charlotte and then next we hear, you've been discovered naked and in bed with her after being shipwrecked in a storm. You propose, she says yes and the tabloids go nuts. Did you borrow this plot from one of your movies?"

Declan snorted because it did sound kind of like a script. "The wreck was an accident."

"And the naked part?"

"None of your business."

His brother laughed. "So the two of you hooked up and then, somewhere along the line, you developed feelings for her, but meanwhile J.J. realized he had a use for her after all because she's a lovely girl who doesn't run around starting naked-picture scandals. You proposed. She said yes. So what went wrong and why are you back here blowing up your life?"

"In exchange for letting her choose the charity we would donate to if we won, she agreed to makeover lessons."

Nash rolled his eyes. "Would you say that Charlotte is bright, attractive, funny with a side of determined? Feel free to fill in the blanks here with your favorite words."

"She's sexy, yeah. Curious. Willing to try new things even when it pushes her way out of her comfort zone. She doesn't like to be the center of attention, so people overlook her. Their loss." He shrugged. "But she's a hell of a woman."

Nash stared at him. "And just to be clear, you told this really amazing person that she needed to *change*? And you somehow thought this would endear you to her?"

He winced. "I was thinking of it more as a dare."

"Dare someone to say something dirty to the person on their left or to eat a banana without hands. Sneak into the next-door mansion and skinny dip in the pool. Take the family helicopter on a joyride. Don't dare someone to be a completely different person, especially if you like the original version."

They'd done all those things and more as teenage boys.

"I made that deal with J.J.," he admitted.

"The one where you proved you'd turned over a wholesome new leaf?" Nash snorted. "Christ, he has this whole vision of what we should be. You'd think he'd have figured out by now that people aren't made to order. He got what he got."

"Yeah. Well. J.J. and I signed a contract and part of the deal was that I'd do the race and rehabilitate my public image. Try to look like a real Masterson."

Nash looked at him. "We are Mastersons."

"J.J.'s still looking for the proof of that."

"Let him." Nash ran a hand over the scruff on his face. "Still doesn't change what we are and I still don't see how that caused you to piss all over your relationship with Charlotte."

"J.J. likes Charlotte. He said she was perfect wife material, that he'd be willing to overlook the race loss and stick to the terms of our deal since I'd *landed her.*"

"Yeah. There's a whole lot wrong there."

"And Charlotte found out. She wasn't happy about it. She asked me to leave. I left."

His brother gave him an assessing look. "We've concluded that you're an idiot, right?"

"Pretty much."

"So let's fix this." Nash spread his arms. "Assuming, based on your behavior in there, that fixing this is your number one priority. Go back. Tell her whatever you need to make this work."

Declan swore. "Can you be more specific?"

"No."

"Great. That's really helpful. What exactly are your relationship credentials?"

Nash shrugged. "I am a doctor."

Nash was one of the smartest, most analytical people Declan knew. He was not, however, a people person. In any way. Declan had always been the one who could connect easily with others. Problem was, those had been surface connections. Between living in the public eye and the constant need to travel for work, he hadn't stuck around in one place for long—certainly not long enough to meet a woman and fall in love.

"You have a PhD in chemistry," he pointed out.

"Yeah, which makes me a chemistry expert," his brother said smugly. "Although if you're having chemistry problems, I don't want to know. She said yes once, though, so that's something."

"Yeah, but then she took it back."

Nash laughed. "You have to learn to close. Remember that cupcake stand we had?"

"We made two hundred bucks." They'd loaded up on dollar-store cake mixes and set up shop in front of J.J.'s Malibu mansion. Declan's job had been to charm everyone into stopping for a closer look, which he'd done. Gardeners, delivery guys, two dog walkers, a rock star and a well-known director. Once he'd delivered them to Nash, Nash had sold the hell out of their cupcakes. His brother was a ruthless negotiator.

"Charlotte seems nice," Nash said.

"She's not interested in the Hollywood lifestyle," Declan said. "Mansions, luxury cars and designer clothes, red carpet time—those things aren't exactly on her bucket list."

Nash leaned forward. "Nothing wrong with those things, but yeah. I get it. She wants something more than icing."

"What the fuck is it with you and the food metaphors?"

Nash groaned. "I *fucking* missed lunch because of your temper tantrum back there. So what does she love? And put some thought into it, okay? Don't just blurt out whatever comes into your head first."

Declan thought, and while he was thinking a taco

truck pulled into the Masterson parking lot. He slid his brother—who was tucking his phone back into his pocket—a glance.

"Everyone should have the taco lady on speed dial," his brother said virtuously.

"Martha's Vineyard, her foster kids, cupcakes. Those are definitely at the top of Charlotte's *like* list."

Nash headed toward the taco truck. "You putting yourself on that list?"

"I screwed up. What if I go back and just screw it up some more?"

Nash sighed and placed his order with the beaming lady manning the taco truck. "You realize I get paid five hundred dollars an hour to consult, right?"

Declan pulled his wallet out and slapped a hundred-dollar bill into his brother's hand. Nash promptly tucked it into the tip jar on the taco truck counter. "Waiting for my advice."

"So here's my suggestion. Do the work to figure out how you make your life fit into hers. The whole cross-country thing is hard. The interest in your personal life is unfortunate because she seemed like the kind of woman who wants to reserve the right to go grab a cup of coffee in her yoga pants, yeah? But then you go there and you actually have a conversation with her. Tell her you still love her and that you want a chance. Ask her what it'll take for her to give you that chance. Then do that."

"That's a pretty simple plan."

"It's authentic." Nash paused. "Also, I'd suggest groveling. Bring her a present that's personal, too, one that shows you've been paying attention to her and that you've got her back. And whatever you do, don't make her feel as if you think that she can't handle her own shit. Just make sure she understands that your goal is to be real with her—and be with her."

Doing those things might actually help. He slid his brother a glance. "How did you get so smart?"

Nash flashed him a rare smile. "Didn't say it worked. This is a working hypothesis only. Go prove it."

Twenty-One

Step one in Charlotte's change-her-life plan: conquer her fear of the ocean. Since the plan also called for accepting her limitations and loving herself as is, the steps were more like baby steps…and had her sitting in a kayak. There was no storm today and no rip current, so she felt optimistic. Or possibly that was because someone had made a large anonymous donation to Martha's Kids. Since the donation had been made on behalf of the "Guinea Pig Appreciation Society," she wasn't entirely clueless about the money's source. Declan had come through for her kids.

The teenager who'd rented her the kayak stared at her dubiously. He was ankle-deep in the water—and all of two feet away from her. "You want a push?"

"No, thanks," she said. "I'm good."

She liked being able to see the bottom. Each time the

wave pushed her kayak onto the shore, she nudged it back out to sea with a careful prod of her paddle.

"Seriously," the teenager said. "Happy to help."

She ignored him because she had thirty minutes left on her one-hour rental and she estimated that was just enough time to make it to the end of the beach and back. And also, because while she was trying to ask for help when she needed it, this situation definitely didn't count. By the time she made the return trip, her face was pink from the sun and her nonexistent core muscles had quit in protest, but she'd done it. And if she felt sad and a little teary, she'd blame that on the bag of M&M's she'd mainlined in the beach parking lot for courage. Unfortunately, it explained why her stomach hurt but not her heart.

She made an ungraceful exit from the kayak, once again grateful that her paparazzi days were behind her. But hey, she was voluntarily in the ocean up to her ankles, so she counted that as a win, and it had been hours—half a day, even—since she'd thought about Declan. She'd moved on from compulsively stalking him on the internet and wondering what he was doing and if she'd really, really screwed up this time.

She dragged the kayak up the sand toward the rental kiosk, feeling kick-ass, if tired. A Hollywood action hero with muscles would almost have been a welcome sight. She would've totally asked him to do the heavy lifting. Instead, she panted and heaved and got the stupid, bright yellow kayak back to its jaded teenage protector, who turned out to be mostly interested in finding out if she really knew Declan Masterson and was the dude coming back any time soon?

She had to admit that she didn't know.

But it was…unlikely.

She shoved that thought out of her head and walked back to her car, pretending her calf muscles didn't ache almost as badly as her heart. Although her hair was twisted up on top of her head, she might have been wearing one of the fancy T-shirts Declan had picked out for her, which was a thousand times better than wearing the shirt she'd stolen from him.

She still wasn't ready to call him, though, or even to text him. *She'd* broken up with him, so she owed him an apology. She had a draft written on her phone. She sort of, completely and impossibly wanted to see him.

And touch him. Hold him. Have him back in her life in all the ways. If wishes were horses, she'd have a large herd.

But sending him on his way had been the right thing to do. She'd thought about it and she stuck by that decision. It wasn't her job to fix Declan and it was okay to have boundaries. Boundaries like not accepting half-truths or being anyone's convenience. Boundaries were good. She'd worked on setting a few with her father.

Funny how she'd had to lose the men she loved in order to learn that lesson. Moving on from the past was surprisingly difficult, but she was taking it one day at a time. *Look at me*, she thought. She'd almost made it an entire day without thinking about him. It was as if her brain had one of those clocks. *It has been one day since the last accidental thought of he-who-shall-not-be-named.*

There was someone leaning against her car—a large, male someone with scruff on his jawline and a small frown on his handsome face. He looked like safety. He looked like home.

And just like that, the Declan Masterson clock reset. *Zero days without a lost time accident.* She sighed.

"Summer camp is on after all because a really big fan of guinea pigs made a huge donation."

The frown turned into a small smile. "That's great."

Right. "You wouldn't know anything about that donation?"

He just looked at her. "It can be from whoever you want it to be from."

"A *million* dollars?"

Warm hazel eyes held hers. "Worth every penny."

"Why?" She inhaled. Exhaled. Reminded herself that people breathed successfully every day.

"I love you."

As reasons went, that one was undoubtedly the best and she really needed to hear him say it again. She tested the words in her head. *I love you.* And look at that: the sky didn't fall, a monster wave didn't swamp the beach and everything seemed perfectly normal. Except—

"You just came back to say that you love me?"

"Yes." And then he paused. "Well, mostly. I needed to tell you that I failed the inheritance test."

"Okay," she said cautiously.

"In fact," he said, "it might be more accurate to say I tore it up and walked out on the examiner." She was no J.J. expert, but she had a gut feeling that Declan's dad had not been happy with that move.

She hesitated. "Declan."

He waited for her to say something more, but she was running on empty.

He solved that problem for her by opening his arms. "Can I hold you?"

"That sounds like a good plan." She squeezed her eyes shut to keep the tears where they belonged and stepped forward. Blindly. But it was all good because Declan had never, ever not held on to her even when she was doing stupid things like falling overboard.

His arms closed around her. "I missed this. I missed you, Charlotte."

"We still wouldn't work."

She felt his mouth brush her hair and when she cracked an eye, he was smiling ruefully.

"Nash said I should make a speech here. He recommended sonnets. But here's the thing. I love you. There aren't any strings attached to that. No expectations. No pretty words. But I would like to spend time with you. Do you think you could make space for me in your life?"

"You want in on my life?" she said softly, opening her eyes because she had to see his face.

"Yeah." He smiled at her. "In your life. In your heart. Whatever you've got for me, I'll take."

"I'm a little short on trust right now," she admitted. "I have a hard time believing Prince Charming is as good as he looks. Or that he's not going to get back on that white horse of his and ride away, with my heart and the good silver in his saddlebags. I'm…" She didn't know how to explain, but she knew she had to try. "I'm a work in progress and I don't know if I want a fairy tale anyhow. I'm going to screw up. I'll never be perfect and I'm working on being okay with that. I'm not sure I'll ever be good at asking for help."

"I don't want you to be anyone other than you," he said. "And I'm not perfect, either."

There were a million things she should be asking him.

Or telling him. Starting with all the reasons why they shouldn't rush into a relationship—*again*—and ending with, well, she didn't know what.

Because face-to-face with Declan, she didn't want to think about endings. *Or that he's still a Prince Charming and you* know *you shouldn't trust those...*

"You haven't asked me why I'm not perfect," he said. "But I'll give you a hint. I told you that I would always hold on, even if it hurt—and then I didn't. You told me to leave and I did. I'd like to prove to you that I'll never let go of you again. You're not window dressing. You're so much more than that."

"Really?"

"Yeah." Cupping her face, he lifted it to his. "I made a plan to get you back. Do you want to see it?" he asked. "I know how you love lists."

What she loved was him.

"Only if you really mean it," she said. "I can't—I don't…"

"It's a heartfelt plan," he said and then he reached into the back pocket of his jeans and pulled out an honest-to-God list.

The list had been rolled up like a scroll and stuck through a ring. *Their* ring. She unrolled the list with trembling fingers. Declan had written in a bold, decisive scrawl:

1. *Tell Charlotte I love her.*
2. *Tell Charlotte I love her.*
3. *Tell Charlotte I love her.*
4. *Buy a house in Martha's Vineyard with a tower. Or at least a turret.*
5. *Love Charlotte forever.*

"I repeated the most important part," he said. "So there's a lot of duplication in my plan because there's only one thing that matters: if I love you and you love me. I have the first part covered, but the second half is all yours. That's what makes this a partnership."

She blinked away tears.

"Just so you know, crying was not part of my plan," he said, his voice full of concern.

"It means your plan is working. And I'm happy."

"And—" he prompted.

"And I love you, too."

* * * * *

Get 4 FREE REWARDS!

We'll send you 2 FREE Books plus 2 FREE Mystery Gifts.

PRESENTS

Unwrapping His New York Innocent

HEIDI RICE

PRESENTS

Forbidden to the Desert Prince

MAISEY YATES

Married By Midnight

SHANNON McKENNA

BRENDA JACKSON THE OUTLAW'S CLAIM

FREE Value Over $20

Both the **Harlequin® Desire** and **Harlequin Presents®** series feature compelling novels filled with passion, sensuality and intriguing scandals.

YES! Please send me 2 FREE novels from the Harlequin Desire or Harlequin Presents series and my 2 FREE gifts (gifts are worth about $10 retail). After receiving them, if I don't wish to receive any more books, I can return the shipping statement marked "cancel." If I don't cancel, I will receive 6 brand-new Harlequin Presents Larger-Print books every month and be billed just $6.30 each in the U.S. or $6.49 each in Canada, a savings of at least 10% off the cover price, or 6 Harlequin Desire books every month and be billed just $5.05 each in the U.S. or $5.74 each in Canada, a savings of at least 12% off the cover price. It's quite a bargain! Shipping and handling is just 50¢ per book in the U.S. and $1.25 per book in Canada.* I understand that accepting the 2 free books and gifts places me under no obligation to buy anything. I can always return a shipment and cancel at any time by calling the number below. The free books and gifts are mine to keep no matter what I decide.

Choose one: ☐ **Harlequin Desire**
(225/326 HDN GRJ7)

☐ **Harlequin Presents Larger-Print**
(176/376 HDN GRJ7)

Name (please print)

Address   Apt. #

City   State/Province   Zip/Postal Code

Email: Please check this box ☐ if you would like to receive newsletters and promotional emails from Harlequin Enterprises ULC and its affiliates. You can unsubscribe anytime.

Mail to the **Harlequin Reader Service:**
IN U.S.A.: P.O. Box 1341, Buffalo, NY 14240-8531
IN CANADA: P.O. Box 603, Fort Erie, Ontario L2A 5X3

Want to try 2 free books from another series! Call 1-800-873-8635 or visit www.ReaderService.com.

*Terms and prices subject to change without notice. Prices do not include sales taxes, which will be charged (if applicable) based on your state or country of residence. Canadian residents will be charged applicable taxes. Offer not valid in Quebec. This offer is limited to one order per household. Books received may not be as shown. Not valid for current subscribers to the Harlequin Presents or Harlequin Desire series. All orders subject to approval. Credit or debit balances in a customer's account(s) may be offset by any other outstanding balance owed by or to the customer. Please allow 4 to 6 weeks for delivery. Offer available while quantities last.

Your Privacy—Your information is being collected by Harlequin Enterprises ULC, operating as Harlequin Reader Service. For a complete summary of the information we collect, how we use this information and to whom it is disclosed, please visit our privacy notice located at corporate.harlequin.com/privacy-notice. From time to time we may also exchange your personal information with reputable third parties. If you wish to opt out of this sharing of your personal information, please visit readerservice.com/consumerschoice or call 1-800-873-8635. **Notice to California Residents**—Under California law, you have specific rights to control and access your data. For more information on these rights and how to exercise them, visit corporate.harlequin.com/california-privacy.

HDHP22R3

HARLEQUIN
PLUS

Announcing a **BRAND-NEW** multimedia subscription service for romance fans like you!

Read, Watch and Play.

Experience the easiest way to get the romance content you crave.

Start your **FREE 7 DAY TRIAL** at www.harlequinplus.com/freetrial.